Haunted

Also by Kim Antieau

Novels

The Blue Tail • Broken Moon • Butch
Church of the Old Mermaids • Coyote Cowgirl
Deathmark • The Desert Siren • The Fish Wife
Her Frozen Wild • The Gaia Websters
Jewelweed Station • The Jigsaw Woman
Maternal Instincts • Mercy, Unbound
The Monster's Daughter
Queendom: Feast of the Saints
The Rift • Ruby's Imagine • Swans in Winter
Whackadoodle Times • Whackadoodle Times Two

Nonfiction

Answering the Creative Call
Certified: Learning to Repair Myself and the World
in the Emerald City
Counting on Wildflowers: An Entanglement
Old Mermaids Book of Days and Nights
The Salmon Mysteries: a Reimagining of the Eleusinian Mysteries
The Salmon Mysteries Workbook: Reimagining the
Eleusinian Mysteries
Under the Tucson Moon

Collections

Entangled Realities (with Mario Milosevic)
The First Book of Old Mermaids Tales
Tales Fabulous and Fairy
Trudging to Eden

Chapbook

Blossoms

Blog

www.kimantieau.com

Haunted

Short Stories

Kim Antieau

Green Snake
PUBLISHING

*In memory of Charles L. Grant,
a superb editor who supported my work
from the beginning.*

Contents

Haunted

Short Stories

Briar Rose

She opened her eyes to white and realized she knew nothing.

The nurse was white, too.

"Good morning, sugar," the nurse said. "Do you know who you are?"

She shook her head and wondered where the window was. Maybe if she saw the sunlight, maybe if she saw the world really existed, she would know. Silly thought. The world existed. It was she, she was certain, who was not supposed to be.

"Turn over," the nurse said. Her voice was as pretty as anything she could remember. Though that wasn't much. She turned over. The nurse threw off the covers and pulled up her hospital gown. "Lookie here, girl," the nurse said. "Maybe that will jar your memory."

She looked down at her own bare ass, twisting her head and arching her back. A small rose bloomed on her white butt, its red petals surrounded by a crown of thorns.

She touched it.

"Maybe my name is Rose," she said.

"All right, Rose, honey," the nurse said, putting the hospital gown and covers back over her bare skin. "We don't know who you are either. You came in with glass all over your arms, cut deep."

Rose held up her bandaged arms.

"You said you'd fallen through a plate glass window." The nurse smiled. "We decided to take your word on that and not put you in the psych ward. All you have to do now is eat that shit they call food, rest, and get better. Just whistle if you need anything."

The nurse in white smiled; for a moment, Rose thought she was dressed in shining armor. Rose shook her head and the nurse was gone. She closed her eyes and reached into her memory. Nothing. Except a man with a needle that looked like those wood burners they used in shop class when she was in high school. "Have you come to be transformed?" the man asked. "I don't think so," she answered. "I just want a rose tattoo." He hummed some tune, Beethoven's Fifth, while he rat-ta-tat-tatted on her backside.

When he was finished, he smoothed a bandage over the patch of skin and handed her a card with care instructions, as if she had just bought a sweater. She pulled up her pants and went home. Home? She couldn't really see it, only her reflection in the mirror, somehow, as she pulled off the bandage and looked at the scab forming where he had drawn the rose with his needle and ink.

"There now," she said. "I am whole again. I am myself. My body is mine."

Rose opened her eyes and started to call to Nurse White, to tell her she did know something. Instead, she closed her eyes again and went to sleep.

In the morning, after she ate the shit they called food, Rose got out of bed, found her bloodstained clothes, and got dressed. She was frightened until she thought of the rose blooming on her butt, and then she was no longer afraid. She walked into the hallway, got on the elevator, and went down to the lobby. Outside through the revolving doors, Rose saw a world she had never seen before, bright, noisy. White with color. No, bright with color. She reached into her pockets as she went down the street, away from the hospital. She pulled out forty dollars, crumpled up in her front pockets. That was it.

She hummed Tchaikovsky's *1812 Overture* as she walked. Pigeons shadowed her as she went down the street, toward the tall buildings and bridges arching the river or expressway. The pigeons dogged her steps, looking for handouts. As she walked she remembered nothing except the rose, knew nothing except the feel of her own skin under her hand. She smiled. Ignorance was bliss.

When she got downtown, the pigeons swore at her and flew away to the Burger King parking lot. Rose went onto a street called Burnside and walked until she came to a door which said: TATTOOS, CLEAN SURROUNDINGS, NO ONE UNDER 18 ADMITTED. Rose gently pulled off the gauze from her arms. Scabs traced the places the glass had cut. She dropped the gauze and scabs into a garbage can and then pushed the door open and went inside.

The man with the wood burner looked up when she came in. He smiled. He was the man from her memory.

"Sorry, honey, I can't take it off."

"I don't want it off," she said. "I want another one." She stepped past the swinging door and into his domain of stencils and needles, inks and memories. She looked at the drawings on his walls.

"You going to pick from my flash this time? Last visit you wanted something no one else had." He stood next to her and pointed. "There, how about another flower?"

She shook her head. "I want a child. Here on my arm. Do you have a child? I need to remember."

"No, but I can draw one," he said. He had curly black hair and tattoos everywhere she could see. A dragon belched smoke up his right arm. Jupiter surrounded by stars rotated on his left arm. A butterfly flew beneath that.

She followed him to the tattoo place behind his drawing table. He wanted her to lie down, she wanted to sit. He hummed as he cleaned her arm with alcohol, let the air dry it, and then drew a little girl. Rose watched his fingers and arm move and knew that she could do it, too. Draw. Sketch her life. After a time, when no one else came into the shop, he stopped and asked her if she liked the little girl he had drawn.

She looked down at her arm. "That little girl is me," she said.

"Yes," he said, "I know."

"I don't remember if I liked her." The girl was smaller than Rose had imagined, two years old perhaps. The man began spreading the inks onto her arm. Then he sewed the girl into her skin with the color. When he finished, it was dark outside and the little girl was blowing out two candles on a blue-frosted cake.

"Someday, Charlie, my brother, some little prick's going to get her," her uncle Bobbie said. "and it'll all be over. That's the way with girls. Dad always said so." He laughed and spilled beer on himself while her mother sliced pieces of cake. Rose looked over at her father and saw the fear in his eyes; she was only two but she saw it, and Bobbie was too young to drink beer, maybe thirteen.

"Are you all right?" The tattooist touched her arm with his fingers. She moved her arm away from him. "Sorry," he said. "You only want to be touched if it hurts."

She looked at the little girl on her arm. Her lips were pursed, forever trying to blow out the candles.

"Can you teach me how to do this?" she asked.

"Transform yourself? Or tattoo?"

"Draw with a needle."

"Do you have any money?"

"Forty dollars and two memories," she said. "I could stay here. Clean up. Do anything else you want."

"Don't scratch your tattoo," he said. He started to hand her the card with care instructions written on it. She stared at him.

"All right," he said. He nodded as if he had known it all along.

"I want another," she said. "The other arm. A snake."

He got up and went to the door and locked it. He pulled the shade down. Then he took a stencil from his flash and returned to her. "Turn around," he said, "so I can work on your other side." He pressed the drawing onto her arm. When he pulled it away, Rose could see the outline of a snake. She stared at the bandage on her other arm and imagined the girl beneath it while the tattooist drew the snake.

When he was finished, he dropped his instruments. "I can't do any more," he said and walked up the steps that led to his loft. She listened to his heavy breathing for several minutes before she got up. She threw out the needle and put away the inks. Then she went into a small office in the back and curled up on a battered couch.

When she awakened, it was still dark. She felt hurried, as if something had to be finished soon. Something she had started and somehow had messed up. She turned on a light over the desk and looked at her arms. Where the glass had pierced her skin were now black lines, jagged shapes tattooed into her arms.

She remembered standing in the motel room, wondering why she was there. Her mother was dead. Too many sleeping pills. Her father was dead. Too many cigarettes. And she was alive. Her body ached. Her body that wasn't hers. The tattoo itched. It had not brought her back from the edge. Something had pricked her, just as her father had feared: men, boys, life. She hurt, as if slivers of glass were tickling her insides. She had raised her fists in anger, wanted to pound on the windows that looked out onto the parking lot, when suddenly she knew how to have peace.

She ended up in the hospital eating shit and getting sponge baths from Nurse White.

She turned her arms around and pulled off the bandage over the little girl and her birthday cake. The scab came off with the bandage. The girl had tears in her eyes. She had heard the conversation, had known her life had changed.

Rose peeled off the other bandage. The snake shed his scab, and Rose was in the backyard of her home, eight years old, bent over a translucent snake skin, wondering where the snake had gone. What an easy life. If you don't like it, just shed it and begin anew. She reached out a finger and touched the skin tentatively. Dry.

"It it's from a poisonous snake you could die." She looked up. Uncle Bobbie. He smiled. All his smiles looked monstrous. She wasn't sure why. He snatched up the snake skin and began running. She went after him, into the woods where the oaks and maples were shedding their leaves. Suddenly his footsteps stopped and she was alone in the woods. Then Bobbie jumped from behind a tree and threw her to the ground, laughing all the time, tossing the snake skin into the air, out of her reach. He pulled off her pants and then his. When it was over, he promised to get her a pony if she didn't tell anyone.

Rose turned off the light. Now she had four memories.

She watched the man prick pictures into other people's skins all day. She took care of his inks and needles and cleaned the floors. At night, she counted his money and gave it to him. He needled her when everyone was gone. A drop of blood tattooed on her right forearm brought Bobbie back to her, brought his smile as he zipped up his pants and she put her hands between her legs. She cried and he told her to shut up. Her parents were afraid to leave her with anyone else except family. Afraid of the outside world. Uncle Bobbie had been right, they would tell each other, there were millions of guys out there just waiting to hurt their child.

A willow tree brought her father back. She leaned her head against his knee. He stroked her hair while he read his newspaper. Her mother knelt in her garden and whispered to the flowers.

"I've never seen anyone heal as quickly as you do," the tattooist told her. He seemed tired, as if he felt it all, too.

She nodded and took the needle from him. "May I try?"

"Don't hurt yourself," he said.

"Isn't that what this is all about?" she asked, holding the needle like a writer holds a pen, poised to express herself.

"No," he said. And he went up the steps. She waited until she heard his heavy breathing, and then she began drawing.

She tried a flower, but it turned into a warped sun, bringing back a summer when she was four and Bobbie was pushing his fingers between her legs while he held onto something between his legs. Rose laughed at his face, funny Bobbie, until her hurt her and she started to cry and wondered where her mother was. The sun was too hot and the flower were dying.

"Momma," she whispered.

She tried tattooing flowers again, this time on her thighs. First violets, then roses, gardenias, rhodies; a garden bloomed on her skin and she was next to her mother in the dirt. Her mother was crying, the tears making paths through the dust on her face. "What's wrong? What's wrong?" Rose asked. She was ten and her throat hurt from trying not to cry. Bobbie lurked in the bushes somewhere, always waiting, and Momma cried.

The tattooist came down the stairs when it was morning. He looked at her thighs.

"You're an artist," he said.

"The agony and the ecstasy?" she said. "I'm my own Sistine Chapel." She held up the needle. "Will you do my back?"

"Why?"

"I have to remember," she said.

"But wasn't it nice before?" he said. "When you knew nothing?"

She shook her head. "I knew nothing when I was two years old and look what happened."

"You hardly scab," he said.

"I go straight to scarring," she said.

She took off her shirt and camisole. She didn't care if he saw her. He poked holes in her back and let the ink soak in, making the memories permanent. They could be wiped from her brain but not from her skin.

"What have you drawn?" she asked when he paused.

"Can't you tell?" he said. "Don't you remember being a kid in the bathtub with your brother or sister? You'd wipe the other guy's back and then put soap on it and draw, usually words, and the other person would have to guess."

"I didn't have any brothers and sisters," she said. "But I do remember a cousin, Mary, and we played together. Sometimes we took baths together when we were real little and we'd do that. Yes, I remember now." It had been nice to touch her and to be touched by her. They were each the other's drawing boards. They got water and soap everywhere. "We floated little plastic ships in the water and pretended we were seeing the world."

"That's what I put on your back," he said.

She got up and went into the bathroom where there was a full-length mirror and looked at herself. Two girls stood on a sailing ship. They held hands and waved to the mermaids in the water. The ship bobbed in the waves. A flag with a rose on it flapped in the breeze.

Rose smiled. Some of the memories were good.

She went back into the room where the tattooist sat.

"You understand that I have to do this," she said.

"Yes," he said. "It's part of what I do. Transformations, remember. It's difficult sometimes."

She nodded.

She drew a lady on her left calf. Her golden hair flowed away from her as she lay on the bed of skin. Her eyes were open but Rose knew she was dead. Her open eyes had surprised Rose. She had died of an overdose of pills. Eaten one at a time.

"Why?" Rose asked as her mother swallowed a little white pill.

"Because I ache," she said. "I've been stabbed in a million places."

Had Bobbie played with her, too?

"I need you to stay," Rose said. She started to cry. Where was her father? At work? The car was with him. Their closest neighbors, the Nelsons, were gone on vacation. She wasn't sure she could reach anyone else. They lived too far from the city. Out in the country where nothing could hurt them. Her mother had ripped out the phone.

"Bobbie's been playing with me," Rose said. She was twelve, desperate. She'd tell her mother, get her to stay.

"What do you mean?" Her mother swallowed four pills this time.

"You know, putting his thing in me," Rose said. Stop it, Mom. Stay with me.

"Tell your father," she said. "He'll protect you."

That was it. That was all her mother had to say to her after all the agony she had been through.

"He promised me a pony," she said.

"I'm so tired," he mother said.

Rose ran downstairs and out the door. She ran into the dusty afternoon and through the woods toward the house Bobbie shared with his parents, farther and farther away from home. He worked in town at night. Maybe he'd be home now. She pounded and pounded on the door. After a while, she heard his voice from deep within the house. He came to the door, half-asleep.

"What are you doing here?" he said.

"It's Momma," she said. "She's taking too many sleeping pills. Please, you've got to do something."

He opened the screen door and she came in. He went to the phone and called the police and an ambulance. She hated him, despised him, hated herself. But he was going to save her mother.

He took her hand, and they went out to his car. He drove her back to her house and together they went upstairs. Her mother lay on the bed, her hair spread out around her, like a golden-haired Snow White waiting for her Prince Charming. Her eyes were open.

Bobbie started to cry. Rose went away. She wasn't certain where she went. Her soul wandered for a time. She thought she had died when she was eight, but she had been wrong. Now she died. Pricked by her mother's death.

She drew a garden on her other leg. Its weeds and thorns twisted around her calf and up her knee. A man stood among the weeds.

"He never let me near him after that," Rose said.

"Who? Your father?" the tattooist asked.

"No," Rose said. Tears stung her eyes. "Bobbie."

She felt like she was going to throw up. "I hated him, but he was all there was. I guess. Momma had left me a long time before she died. And my dad was . . . my dad."

The tattooist took the needle. Rose lay on her stomach, and he drew on her back. Her butt became a tangle of dark briar that went up her back, no way to get through.

She remembered leaving her bedroom window open. The boys knew where to come in and they did, one at a time. She didn't care who they were. She just opened her legs to them. She had to fill the emptiness somehow.

The briars pricked her skin; the tattooist drew drops of blood down her legs.

She touched the blood and remembered being seventeen. Her father was drunk. She had never seen him drunk before. But he was blind with grief. He wept and started calling her Joanie. Her mother's name. She went into the bathroom and curled her hair up and behind her, dabbed her cheeks with powder, put her mother's pearl necklace around her neck, slipped into her mother's blue flowered dress, the one her mother had worn often, especially when she was in the garden, and then she went out to her father. In the darkness, she opened herself to him, not understanding, and he pushed into her, sobbing, until in the middle of it, hard inside her, he opened his eyes and screamed with the horror of it, knowing it was Rose; knowing it, he kept going. When he was finished, he curled up on the floor and asked how she could have done it.

"Does it hurt?" the tattooist asked.

"Yes." Rose wiped her tears and sat up. "I want you to do my breasts."

He drew flowers and restaurants and neon lights and cowboys. It hurt. He drew her trek across the country after her father told her to leave. She went to Bobbie's house first. He had a wife and a child and he could not look at her. Rose turned away from the house and hoped he never touched his little girl the way he had touched her. She took a ride from a trucker. She let him have her at night, after they drove several hundred miles. She felt dry inside, and he told her she wasn't much fun. "I don't want nobody don't want me," he said. He let her out in the darkness. The next one beat her up. The tattooist pricked the black and blue spot on her skin. She hadn't minded the beatings so much. She deserved it. Touching was meant to hurt. She ended up working in a restaurant in Tucson, fifteen hundred miles from home. For some reason, she told Bobbie where she was.

She looked down at her breasts and saw the envelope, saw the writing on the letter. The tattooist bit his lip as he pushed the needle into her.

"It's for my own good," she said.

"It's for your death," he said.

She nodded.

The letter told her her father was dead. A year to the day she had left. Lung cancer. She didn't go back for the funeral. She stayed in Tucson. A cactus grew from her navel. An old Indian woman tried to heal her insides. But she couldn't let the woman touch her. Couldn't let anyone touch her.

When she turned nineteen, she went north. She found the tattooist and had him etch a rose into her body. It was her body now.

He painted the house around her side. It wrapped her. She had never gone back to the house. She had heard they sold it. Another family lived in it now. After she got the rose, she thought it would be better. It was supposed to be better. A reason to go on: because she had reclaimed her body. Instead, she stood in the motel room and wanted to die.

The tattooist moved away from her. He was crying.

"There are scabs all over your body," he said.

She was naked except for the tattoos.

"Are you glad you remembered?" he asked.

"No," she said. "Thank you."

"Don't go, he said. "You're very good. An artist. You could transform people."

"I can't even transform myself," she said. She put on her clothes. Her entire body hurt.

"I could help you get started," he said. She was quiet. "Stay until the scabs are gone then."

"All right," she said. "I'll at least stay the night."

He started to touch her arm, but he stopped. "I'm going to bed," he said. He slowly walked up the steps to his loft.

Rose went to the office and sat on the couch. Her body was now covered with her memories. It ached with them. She took off her shirt; the throbbing lessened somewhat. She wanted to cry. The memories burned her skin. Hurt. Too much. She stood up and took off her pants. How could she live with it all? Stand it? She touched one of the faces on her body that was Bobbie. He peered at her from her right shoulder. She shook herself, like a dog shaking water from its fur, and the scabs fell away from her body, becoming flower petals, red, yellow, blue, floating slowly to rest on the carpet. Now she could clearly see all her memories. Her life was etched into her skin. She went into the bathroom and stared at her body in the mirror. Her ruined body. Bobbie had ruined her. Killed her. Doomed her to sleep until she died. Her mother had ruined her. Her father had ruined her. She had only been a child. They had all taken pieces of her and had forgotten to give them back.

She started to cry. She thought of those hours when she hadn't remembered anything. When Nurse White had turned her over. A babe from the womb. Being cared for, loved, patted. She had known nothing. Now she knew everything.

Bobbie drank too much. His wife had left him. Her father was dead, never forgiving her. Never realizing it had been his responsibility, not his daughter's. Her mother was dead. Never caring what she left behind.

"Time to wake up," Rose whispered to her reflection.

She reached down and pulled a briar away from the patch that circled the rose on her butt. Her skin itched. Crackled. She sat on the floor and pressed the thorn into the top of her head until she drew blood. It had been good to remember. Blood ran into her eyes. To realize she had only been a child. Her mother had chosen to die; Bobbie had chosen to hurt her; her father had chosen to blame her. It was past. Time for reclamation. Seeing it all had made it, somehow, understandable. She remembered touching the snake skin when she was a child, being amazed that it could just start fresh, shed its old life.

She stretched and creaked and rubbed herself along the carpet, and her past started to fall from her. She sat up and helped it: she peeled away the dead skin. It felt dry and cool, just as the snake skin had. Lifeless. No power. The flowers came away, Bobbie's face, her mother's eyes, the weeds, the ship on her back, the snake, the blood. All of it. She stood and dropped the past onto the carpet. She shook herself, causing the last pieces of skin to fly away. She looked down at her body. She was white and pink. New. Only the rose on her buttock remained, without the crown of thorns.

The tattooist stood in the doorway. He leaned over and picked up the skin.

Rose touched his arm. "Leave it," she said. "I don't need it anymore." She reached down and smoothed her hand over her rose tattoo and smiled. "I am myself again."

Listening for the General

I hear the General below, his shears squeaking open and shut, open and shut, as I search his upstairs room. The noise stops, and I pause. Ice hits crystal, a familiar, penetrating sound, and I know Susano has brought the General his glass of water with lime. I open drawers, peer behind potted ferns, run a broom under the bed. If anyone passes by, I will become the old cleaning woman everyone sees when they look at me, harmless and above suspicion.

The shears open and close again. I glance outside. Pink petaled flowers fall slowly to the ground, brushing the General's shoes silently. I smile. He oils the shears often, and I wipe the oil away: I want his shears to be like the bell around a cat's neck. I hear footsteps downstairs. I push the broom back and forth on the beige and burgundy rug, sending dust into the air. But no one comes.

The shears stop. The outside spigot creaks open. Water splashes tile as the General washes the garden from his hands before his swim. "Susano!" he calls. Footsteps. Soft grunts as the General undresses. I imagine him balanced on the edge of the turquoise-tiled pool. The sound of his body hitting the water is startling, like a watermelon striking concrete.

I complete my search, finding nothing. I have been in the

General's house for a month; still, I know little more about him than when I arrived. He has few visitors and corresponds with no one. Yet I have heard my people screaming in the mountains because of him. I have watched them die of wounds I could not heal. It is said a traitor whispers our secrets to the General.

I have found no traitor, but I will not return to my village until I do.

The General laughs and splashes once, and then the day falls silent again.

The howlers whistle in the amanta tree like possessed children. A breeze twists its way through the tangled gray branches of the enormous tree, becoming an eerie accompaniment to the monkeys. The General stands in the clearing, staring up at the moon whose light washes away the color of his face and clothes. He is silent, yet when the howlers stop for a moment, I think I can hear him breathing the jasmine-perfumed air.

I wonder if he talks to the moon. Perhaps she is the one who tells him the plans of my people; perhaps she urges him to slice away the ear of an enemy or to leave boys disemboweled for the pigs to eat.

The turkeys do not sleep this night. Deep clicking sounds come from their throats as they pick worms and insects off tobacco leaves. A pig shuffles in the dirt. I turn from the General and look at the mountains blackened with night. In those mountains, my people now sleep, dreaming of times they have never known. Their dreams whisper to me, touching my ears with longings for the General's death. Yet his death would only speed along the advancement of another general, someone worse perhaps; and still we would not know who betrays us. I hear the General come toward me. I do not move. I could end him now with the knife I have hidden in the folds of my skirt. I remain still.

"What are you doing, old woman?" he asks, his voice low,

the sound moving up from his chest. These are the first words he has spoken to me.

I turn to him and smile my old woman smile.

"Listening to the music of the howlers, General," I say. "I hope I have not disturbed you."

He stares at me for a moment and then looks at the amanta tree.

"Music? You call that screeching music?" he asks, staring at the ghost-colored branches. He shakes his head. "No, you have not disturbed me. There are traitors everywhere, so I must be careful. You listen to monkeys? Well, listen for me, old woman, listen for the traitors."

The howlers are quiet, and I wonder if they understand us.

"I am an old woman," I say, "and sometimes I cannot even hear my own thoughts."

He laughs and the howlers imitate him. His laughter dies away and he looks back at the tree, squinting.

"Someday I shall shoot them all," he says, and then his feet bend the dry grass, making it crackle like fire licking tender branches as he walks back toward the house.

Through the chink in the door I observe the woman from the city sitting across from the General. She sips champagne quietly. The General drinks his champagne continuously; the sound is like a pig with its nose buried deep in the stomach of a corpse. The light from the chandelier cleanses the room and accents the woman's diamonds and white satin dress. She is very young. I hear a clicking sound, and when I lean forward from my hiding place on the stairway, I see the General tapping his medals with the nails of his right hand.

"Most people believe I received these because I was either brave or brutal," he says. His knife scrapes across his plate as he cuts into his steak. "Both are true, of course, but not important.

What is important to my success is that I have not forgotten the ways of the old ones. The rebels and terrorists in the mountains talk about getting their people food and putting shoes on their children's feet. It is all nonsense. The children are better off with their feet in contact with the Earth. They should be grateful to me. I could be harder on them, but I am not an extremist. I am able to keep order for the President by making only occasional raids. I am able to keep order because I remember the ways of our people. Others would be wise to remember the old ones, too.

"I will show you," he says. The cupboard door creaks slightly, sounding like the General's yawn as it moves open. Paper crinkles. The woman picks up the nutcracker—I see her rings flash as she reaches across the table. She places the nut between the metal bars, and then the shell cracks into a million pieces that scratch my ears, bringing my nightmare into this waking time. I close my eyes and the sound reverberates. I hear my nephew's screams again as the machete descends on him and slices through cartilage. His ear drops to the ground in an almost inaudible swoosh. I hear the smile in the General's voice as he orders one of his men to pick up the ear. I wait behind bamboo walls, listening to my own breath and the moans of my nephew until the sound of hooves dies away. The woman cracks open another nut, and tears touch my cheeks.

I hear the rustling of paper again and then something drops into liquid. I lean forward. The General's holding a paper sack. Something brown, like a dried peach, floats in the woman's champagne.

"I know the ways of the old ones," he says, "and I listen well. They all wonder why I take only one ear, or why I do not kill all the men outright instead of taking an ear. They don't understand." He laughs; it is more like a gurgle, like someone choking in water. The woman has grown pale and her skin now matches her dress. "I hear everything if I listen closely enough. I hear their thoughts, I hear the moans of their lovers, I hear the secrets of their comrades. I even hear the worms eating them as they lie buried beneath the ground."

I move back into the darkness, not wanting to see the thing floating in the glass or hear it take in champagne like a sponge soaking up water.

How foolish we all were. We have called the General many things, but we never thought of him as one of us. We had forgotten he is of our race, he is a human being. I shudder. He is also someone who serves the old gods, an *ah-men*—or more likely, an *ah-pulyaah,* a practitioner of black magic. Or so the outsiders name it. His trick is an old one: if an *ah-pulyaah* takes an eye, he can see all that the other eye sees, if he takes a hand, he'll know what the other hand does. If he slices off an ear, it becomes a cornucopia of thoughts and sound.

The General comes to the door, and I press myself against the wall. The light is shut away as the door closes tightly. I stand and leave the house, my feet making no more sound than mist does as it settles on the tube roses. I hope the General does not hurt the woman from the city, but I am afraid he saw the fear in her eyes, just as I did.

I scrape bark from the amanta tree and drop the shavings into my bag. The howlers hiss at me. The night is quiet except for a faraway wind pushing trees against the mountainsides. Back in the darkened kitchen, I poke at the fire until it snaps at me, and then I boil the bark. The sounds of bubbles breaking fills the room. Then I wait for the liquid to cool. The house is silent as I stir honey into the bark. My father was an *ah-men* and I used to listen to his chants as a child. His words were not for female ears, and his black magic was something he practiced only occasionally. Yet I had listened. Later I sometimes used the knowledge when I was needed as a healer; the Lords of the Days always served me, apparently unaware of my sex.

I take the newly made *balché* out to the amanta tree, and there I drink it slowly. The turkeys pick, pick, pick. When the monkey howls turn to lullabies and the sun begins to rise, I take out my father's *zaztiin,* a clear stone ball given to him by his father, and I dip it in the *balché.* I chant softly.

The distant hills are bathed in smoky purple. The air surrounding the estate is tinged in gold. A car takes away the woman from the city. I hear her tears as they fall into her palm, like drops of water falling from the tallest tree in the rain forest to the forest floor. The General goes to the garden and begins his day. The shears squeak open and shut. A breeze brings the words of Susano to me as he asks Julia where the old woman is. Ice clicks against crystal. Water hits tile. The General laughs and splashes in the pool.

I drink *balché* and wait for the sun to drop again. When it is dark, the monkeys chatter noisily, as if to hide the sounds of my soles as I go into the kitchen. I drop a large portion of sleeping powder into the General's night drink just before Susano comes for it. Then I take a butcher knife from the kitchen and wait outside with the monkeys, sharpening the blade, until the house grows silent with sleep.

Ferns brush my cheeks as I walk up the stairs. Inside the General's room, I scratch matches against metal. The flame hisses and bursts gold. I light the lantern. The flame spits at me as it illuminates the General's face. I dab the skin around his ear with alcohol. He does not move.

I put the blade to his ear, and then swiftly, I force the knife down. For a moment, I hear sounds like a machete slicing through cornstalks; the room glows gold and I am not certain where I am, and then the ear falls away from the General's head. I watch black liquid stain the sheets and hear it seep into the linen like misty rain falling on soldier's fatigues. I wrap his head with bandages. The General moans once. I place his ear on one of his silk handkerchiefs. Then I pull out the *zaztiin* and wave it over the ear. The clear stone squeaks on its chain like the General's shears. My chants fill the house. I hear them travel outside where the monkeys repeat my words.

When I am certain the Lords of the Days have heard me, I wrap the ear in the handkerchief. I listen to the General's uneven breathing. Now we shall know his thoughts, too; his ear will be better than the warning bell on a cat. I go downstairs and get the paper sack from the dining room. The only sound is the crackling of the paper against my hand. I imagine the ears pressed against the sack, listening.

I leave the house and take a horse from the stables. I ride past the amanta tree where the monkeys click and past the tobacco field where the turkeys gobble worms. I hold the ear close to mine to hear the General's dreams. His dream sounds are empty—like splashes of water in a turquoise-tiled pool. The horse knows the mountain well and it carries me quickly toward my village. I am not afraid of the dark because I know the General's men do not come out at night. Insects snap at the ear, drawn to its sound like moths to a light. The General's dreams keep me company through the night.

The sun lights the sky as I arrive at my village. People gather round me, offering food and drink. I had not told any of them where I had gone. Now they question me. I listen to the ear, and the sounds of the General's screams come to me. He has discovered his loss.

"This is the General's ear," I say, sliding off the horse.

"Only his ear, grandma?" one of the villagers says as I open the handkerchief. "Is he dead?"

I shake my head. "I have done better than kill him."

Suddenly everything becomes quiet. I look around. I hear tortillas sizzling, a dog barking, my horse's urine spraying the ground, yet it is quiet. I gaze down at the ear in my hand, and I realize I am no longer hearing the sounds which accompanied me to the village. The General is silent.

We hear news of the *Matanza*—the slaughter—long before it reaches us. The General is no longer content with taking parts of us, we are told; instead, he is killing us all. I wave my *zaztiin* over his shriveled ear and call up the Lords of the Days. They do not listen. The young people either laugh at me or curse me for letting the General live as they make preparations to leave their homes.

I am inside my hut when the General rides into the village. His horses breathe hard, sucking in the dusty day. The soldiers' guns bang against their legs, making a strange metallic thud. I peer through the bamboo walls. The General sits on his palomino, his head turned away from me. I can see the scar where I cut off his ear. It has healed nicely. He twists his head around. The other scar has not healed as well. It is ragged and red where he cut—or tore-off—his ear. Now I understand why the Lords did not hear my chants.

The General motions to his men and the screaming begins. As I run from my house, I hear his head move, the bones in his neck cracking, and I know he is looking at me.

"Old woman!" he screams, his words twisting into the howls of the monkeys who sit like ghosts in the old amanta tree. His words fill my ears as the sounds die all around me.

Mourning Period

The Boston fog was spotty, one minute enveloping the taxi Tara and Calder traveled in and the next gone, revealing how fast the cab was going. Tara closed her eyes and willed herself to relax. Tomorrow, her car would be fixed.

Calder was quiet next to her, untroubled. He took his wife's hand in his. He knew she wanted to be driving. To be in control. We'll be home soon, he told her with the gentle pressure of his hand. He leaned over and kissed her.

And then they were flying through the mist. The driver swore as the car tumbled over the embankment. Tara flung herself in front of Calder protectively. Metal met earth, and glass shattered and came to rest in the bodies of the dead, save one.

The house had settled crookedly and comfortably in the damp Oregon soil. Mold grew unchecked on baseboards and windows. In the distance, Calder heard the soothing sound of water meeting land. Fresh air wafted in through the open front door, bringing with it the moist briny scent of the ocean. It was a pleasant smell that reminded him of Tara and their life in Boston. Boston was three thousand miles away and Tara three months dead.

His sister Lisa dangled keys in front of him.

"It's going to take a lot of work," she said. "No one has lived here in over a year. Are you sure you don't want me to take you shopping or anything?"

"I'm sure, " he said.

Lisa followed him as he wandered through his new home.

"You're going to be so isolated," she said. "You are going to get a phone, aren't you?"

He shrugged. Who would he call?

"I came here to be alone," he reminded her. "I have neighbors if I do want company." He wouldn't be able to find a permanent teaching job in such a small town, at least not for a while, but he didn't care. He had enough insurance money to allow him to sit by the ocean and take up painting again. He could substitute teach for extra money.

He stopped at the bathroom and peered inside. The bathtub was the huge old freestanding kind Tara loved. She used to write her briefs in their bathtub in Boston, swearing whenever a page dropped in the water or smiling up at him when he came in to leer at her. He could almost see her now, her shiny black hair pinned on top of her head, her hand reaching up for him. . .

"Calder?" Lisa said. "Did you hear me? I've got to get home."

She hugged him; he returned the embrace absently. When she pulled away, he saw she was crying.

"We all miss her," she said. She hurried out of the house and got into her car and drove away.

Calder was alone for the first time in ten years.

She had always known she would not want to be alive if anything happened to Calder. It was not that she couldn't handle things on her own. It was just that she was happy with him, unhappy without him. They complemented one another. She saw herself as a revolutionary working through the system, always ready for the good fight. She watched the world and its leaders and believed fervently, despite all evidence to the contrary, that the world could be saved and joined in unity. Calder, on the other hand, had no real interest in the world as a political entity. Instead, he believed in the individual and he taught children how to make choices. Or so he always told Tara when she attempted to inspire or anger him with tales of the injustices of the world. Tara envied his stoicism.

He calmed her with his steadiness, and she had loved him for thirteen years. After she finished her undergraduate work, he waited for her while she went to Africa for two years in the Peace Corps. When she returned, they got married. She went to law school; Calder continued teaching. She had envisioned sixty more years with him at least. Thus, when faced with his death on that taxicab ride home, she had thrown her body across his, her effort to save his life. And it had. He was alive.

She wasn't.

Yet she had not left him, she told herself, as she looked down at her sleeping husband, his arm stretched across the empty pillow next to him. She was with him in this strange house on the Oregon coast. She bent over to kiss him. It was a useless gesture. She could feel nothing.

"Tara," her husband whispered, still asleep. Tara slipped out of the house and down to the beach. Calder had made a good choice. It was a lovely beach. She liked the huge rocks strewn in and out of the water, slowing the colliding waves before they reached shore. She wished she could walk barefoot, let her feet get so cold the water would begin to feel like glass pricking at her soles. But that was all gone. It had to be enough that she was even there.

Calder was drawn to the ocean. He would sit in his studio trying to paint, and suddenly he had to leave. After dropping his sketch pad into his shoulder bag, he would quickly walk the quarter of a mile to the beach. Once there, he would sit on his favorite rock and watch the waves and think of Tara and how much she loved the ocean. Out to sea, at massive Table Rock, the waves mounted, became a wall of blue—or, more often, gray or dirty green—and then crashed against the rock, spilling foam in all directions. Sea gulls sat atop the rock, perhaps as mesmerized as he. Sometimes the waves were so high that the foam sprayed to the top of the rock, taking on quick mysterious shapes. There was a hand reaching for a sea gull, a baton twirling in the autumn wind, a woman in white bending to the sea.

One night, Calder went down to the beach during a full moon. He surprised himself, walking in the dark alone. Once he stepped onto the beach, he forgot his aloneness and saw a world transformed. A mist hung in the air like a web in a dimly lit closet. The sea was quiet, the waves almost languid. Moonlight lay across a patch of rippled sand lined like skin. Shapes in the sand more closely resembled sleeping human figures than the bunches of kelp he knew them to be. He gazed out to sea where the moonlight touched Table Rock.

At the edge of the water, a woman stood looking toward him. He blinked, and she was gone. A lone sea gull screeched nearby and took to the air, startling Calder. He stayed for a while longer, letting the mist cover him, hoping for another glimpse of the woman.

At first, Tara contented herself with following Calder around, watching him paint, and sitting with him on the rock and looking out to sea. When she saw Calder was not recovering from her death very well, she decided to gradually let her presence be known to him. She could create noises but they were not pleasant sounds, and she didn't want to frighten Calder. She could make things move and herself appear slightly visible. She felt more powerful near the ocean, so it was there she first let Calder see her. When he didn't recognize her, she wanted to run to him, tweak his ear, and say, "Look, it's your wife. Don't you recognize me in my present ethereal state?" She laughed and waved to him. He sat watching, looking puzzled.

One day, as Calder sat in his studio putting the last touches on an ocean scene, Tara made herself visible as a patch of shadow near the windows. Calder looked up.

"It's you, Tara," he said, "isn't it?"

He sniffed the air. The ocean smell had become more intense.

"Tara," he whispered, breathing deeply.

"You've been here two months," Lisa said, blowing steam from her teacup, "and you haven't talked to anyone."

"Not true," he said. He sipped his coffee. "I'm subbing at the schools. I've met some people. I've even invited one of the teachers, Sam Kelly, and his sister and her daughter for dinner next week." He'd done it on the spur of the moment when Sam told him their mother had recently died and his sister, Julie, was not handling it well.

"You haven't written to anyone," Lisa said. "Tara's parents called me the other night to see if you were all right. They were afraid to call you. They're still pretty broken up about Tara's death."

"You should tell them Tara is all right," he said. He looked out the window and wished Lisa would leave. The rain was coming down so hard it was blurring the colors of the day. It was like watching a painting slowly melt into the ground. "I'm sure she's happy wherever she is."

Lisa arched an eyebrow. "Oh? I didn't know you believed in the afterlife."

He shifted in his chair. He was not going to tell her about Tara.

She would not believe him, and she would not understand how much the pain had diminished since Tara had come back. It was so much better than not having her at all.

"I just sense she's okay," Calder said. "That's all."

"OK."

Suddenly, he had to leave. He had to be with Tara. He couldn't stand to sit with his sister for one more minute.

"I'm going for a walk," he said. He grabbed his raincoat, didn't wait to hear any protests from his sister, and left the house.

The rain clapped noisily on his slicker as he hurried toward the beach. He didn't care about the rain. He wanted Tara. Besides, the cold would make a hot bath even more delicious later. He and Tara used to play out in the snow in Boston, getting cold and wet, and then they'd come home and sit in the steamy bathtub, sipping wine and making love.

Calder trotted down the zigzag path to the beach, anxious to find Tara. After their bath, they would make a fire, drink more wine, and make love again. He broke into a run and headed for his rock. He wanted her. He wanted to feel her against his back, curled up to him like a second skin. He wanted to be inside her, to press his chest against hers, to listen to her heartbeat.

He stopped abruptly. The water lapped at his shoes, covered them, and rolled backward. He bit his tongue so he wouldn't cry out. He saw the flicker of Tara's presence. With a sudden surge of agony, he remembered what he had chosen to forget: He could never touch her again. Ever.

"I'm looking forward to having Sam and his family over," Calder told Tara. He took a finished painting from the easel and slid on another canvas. He would have to do something about his backlog of paintings soon. Either give them away or see if he could sell them.

"His sister has a daughter, Melanie," he said. "I guess Julie's divorced and living with Sam for now. She's a freelance writer. Sam's a nice guy. You'll like him."

The house was silent, yet Calder sensed Tara. Sometimes he knew what she was feeling: wonder when they went to the ocean together, love when he read to her as he sometimes did, sympathy for him when Lisa visited. Now he felt nothing from her.

The house shook from a sudden wind. Calder pulled on a sweater, feeling suddenly chilled.

Tara slowly left the house. She wandered outside, rattling the windows almost without knowing it. She saw Calder's figure through the fogged windows, a ghostly undefined shape, looking up when the windows moved. She was glad he had found company, she supposed. When she was alive, she always had lots of friends. Now she only wanted Calder, and he needed other people.

Calder baked chicken in garlic and cut up vegetables for a salad. It was one of Tara's favorite dishes. She wished she could smell it. The doorbell rang, and Calder went to answer it.

Julie was nearly as tall as Calder, with black hair that fell in waves to her shoulders. Her eyes were bluer than any Tara had ever seen and her smile was friendly. A small child, about five, followed Sam and Julie into the house.

"Is anything wrong?" Julie asked Calder after Sam introduced them.

Calder shook his head. "I'm sorry. You just reminded me of someone."

Sounds of people talking and eating filled the house. Tara watched from afar. Calder laughed with the family. After dinner, he lifted Melanie onto his lap while he drank coffee. He took Julie and Melanie to his studio when Sam ran to the car for a forgotten bottle of wine. Julie picked up a framed photograph of Tara.

"Is this who I reminded you of?" she asked. "Was she your wife?"

"Yes, that's Tara," he answered. "You reminded me of her for a second, but don't take it personally. For the first month after the accident, everyone reminded me of her."

"It's awful to lose someone that close," Julie said.

Awful wasn't the world, Calder thought. *Terrifying. A loneliness so overwhelming you're afraid you'll fall in and never return. So you'll settle for anything.*

Melanie tugged on her mother's leg and Julie picked her up.

"I know the feeling," she said. "I still think I see my mother walking down the street about once a week. I wonder when you really know they're dead?"

"When you realize you can't ever touch them again," Calder said.

Tara moved closer to them. She did not like Julie. She was standing too close to Calder. And this business of Julie looking like her was nonsense. Julie's hand brushed Calder's when she set down the photograph. She smiled at him.

"Mommy, it's cold in here," Melanie said.

"She's right," Julie said, hugging Melanie closer to her. "It is suddenly very chilly in here."

Sam came into the room holding a bottle of wine. "This will warm some of us up a bit," he said.

They all laughed and left the studio. Tara moved outside into a cold she could not feel. They don't know how lucky they are, she thought as she went toward the ocean.

Calder's sleep was broken that night. He knew Tara wasn't in the house, and he missed her. And he kept feeling Julie's skin against his, accidentally touching when he passed the salad, shaking hands good-night. He dreamed of her. She came into his room, and he took off her clothes, slowly, kissing her neck and breasts, cupping her buttocks in his hands. She moved over him, dark and naked, a body of warmth and reality. Her eyes flashed blue in the darkness, like lights on the ocean blinking on and off.

"Tara," he whispered to her, forgetting she was Julie. The lights went out in her eyes and she was cool under his hands and then white ice, evaporating into mist, leaving him shivering and alone.

He awoke suddenly, smelling the ocean. Slightly comforted, he fell asleep again and had no more dreams.

As he was putting on his jacket to go down to the beach the next day, someone knocked on his door.

"Julie," he said after he opened the door. "This is a nice surprise."

"I was going for a walk on the beach," she said, "and I thought you might like to come along."

"Funny you should ask," he said. "I was just leaving."

He stepped outside and closed the door behind him. They walked together silently. The autumn sky was clear and blue. After a few minutes, they reached Calder's favorite rock. He hauled himself up. Julie followed, and they sat next to one another. Calder looked around and sniffed the air, but he couldn't tell if Tara was near. Julie was warm next to him, a pleasant, unfamiliar sensation. Water splashed around the rock.

"I like coming here," she said. "I forget about my mother being dead when I'm here."

"Were you close?"

"She was my best friend," she answered, "especially after my husband left. Then we moved in with Sam. It was nice. Where you and your wife happy?"

"Very."

They were quiet for a few minutes.

"Julie," he said suddenly, "would you mind telling me about yourself? From the beginning."

"It's not all that exciting," she said.

"It doesn't matter," he said. "I just want to hear someone else's voice." He leaned against the rock and listened to her soft husky voice as she began her story.

When he went home again, the house was freezing. He turned on all the electric heaters, but he could not shake the chill.

"Tara," he called. "I know ghosts can make cold, but can you make warmth? Do your stuff, lady; I'm freezing."

The house was silent.

"Did you do this?" he asked.

Silence. He sighed. "Are you mad because I took Julie to our rock? Come on, you've never been the possessive type. You should understand."

Still nothing.

"I'm going to read for a while," he said. "Out loud."

He liked to read to her; it was as though they were really doing something together. He picked up a book of Emily Dickinson's poems and began reading. Gradually, the house got warm again.

A couple of days later, Julie came over again. She sat restlessly at Calder's kitchen table.

"It's Mom's birthday today," she said. "I kept thinking she was in my room last night. I wanted her there, but I wanted her gone. Do you know what I mean?"

Calder stood at the counter, kneading dough for bread and letting Julie talk. She had her back to him. She looked so much like Tara from behind; it was eerie. He wished she would turn to face him.

"I didn't realize until after she died that I don't have any friends," she said. "She was such a good friend to me. She was my best critic."

Calder remembered reading Tara's briefs for her. She would spend hours on them, rewriting one passage again and again to subtly sway the evidence toward her point of view. She would have him read them and then ask, "Would you rule in my favor?"

"Sure," he'd invariably answer, "but I've seen you naked."

She would grab the papers from him and hit him over the head with them. Then she'd fall into his lap, laughing. He liked the feel of her buttocks against his groin. Her warmth would spread through his body like a shot of good whiskey on a cold day.

Now Calder wiped his hands on his apron and spread a damp cloth across the dough to let it rise again.

Julie turned to him. "I'm sorry I'm dumping all of this on you," she said.

Calder went to her and put his hands on her shoulders.

"Don't worry about it," he said. "Talk all you want. It makes me forget."

She reached for his hand. He leaned over and kissed her. She was soft and warm. He kissed her again, pulling her to her feet. It had been so long.

"Tara," he whispered.

He smelled brine and suddenly realized Julie was struggling with him, trying to get away. He let her go and stepped back from her, horrified.

"Julie," he said. "Jesus, I'm sorry."

She sank into the chair.

"I'm not Tara," she said.

"I know," he said. He wanted to touch her again, gently, and show her he had not meant any harm. "I've never been unfaithful to her. I don't know what happened."

"Unfaithful? Calder, it was just a kiss," she said. She looked up at him. "My God, you're talking about her as if she were alive. She's dead, Calder." She stood.

"Please don't go," he said. "I'm sorry."

She shook her head and quickly left the house.

Calder woke in the night feeling like he was suffocating from heat. He threw off the covers and stumbled to the heater. It was turned up all the way. He ran around the house. All the heaters were on and the refrigerator door was open.

"Jesus, Tara, this is no way to communicate."

Tara was outside, watching Calder go from heater to heater. He looked silly, running around in his underwear, bumping into things. It was funny that she had never noticed he was silly-looking. And clumsy. He had stubbed his toe twice. Now he was stepping in water from the refrigerator, swearing. What a comic figure. She howled with laughter.

Calder looked around, startled. He had never heard such an awful noise. He closed the refrigerator door. He would clean it up tomorrow. By the time he got back to bed, the house was cold. He turned up his electric blanket and lay wide-eyed in bed.

"What's going on, Tara?"

The silence vibrated around him, and he knew he was alone.

In the morning, the house felt warm and cheerful. The floor in front of the refrigerator was dry.

"Is this your way of making up?" he asked as he made breakfast. He heard a noise in the living room and went to check on it. A book had fallen from the shelf. He smiled.

"All right, after breakfast I'll read," he said. As he walked back to the kitchen, he realized they had just had their first fight.

Julie called the next day to invite Calder for Thanksgiving dinner.

He hesitated.

"I don't want you to feel bad about what happened," Julie said. "I was just upset because . . . you called me Tara."

"I know," he said. "I acted a little strange and I'm sorry."

"I'm not really sure how dinner will turn out," she said.

"We've had some strange things happen in the past few days. The stove won't turn off unless we unplug it. And the furnace keeps coming on in the middle of the night and toasting us."

"What?" Calder felt suddenly frightened.

"Sam thinks the house has become haunted," Julie said.

"I don't believe it," he whispered. *Tara.*

"What's wrong?" she asked.

"Nothing, don't worry about it," he said. "I'll talk to you later." He hung up the phone and looked around the room.

"How can you do things like that to other people?" Calder said. "They haven't done anything to you." He slowly sat on the couch.

Tara became a patch of mist near the window. Couldn't he see what a little slut Julie was? *You don't need them, you have me.*

"I've got to have other people," he said.

I gave you your life, she shrieked, knowing he wouldn't understand her.

"Why did you have to save me anyway?" he asked. "How do you know we wouldn't both have survived that crash if you'd stayed where you were? You always had to have things your way. Control them."

If I hadn't controlled things, where would you be now?

"When you were alive, it didn't matter," he said, "because you did other things that balanced that out your tendencies to try to control everything. You're different now, Tara. Don't you see it?"

Stupid man. Tara roared. The house shook. Windows rattled almost to the point of breaking.

"Tara, don't do this," Calder said.

Calder woke up struggling against unseen hands. He bolted upright, pulling covers away from his face.

"Tara?" The house was quiet. Tara would not hurt him. He

must have been tossing in his sleep. He lay back and pulled the covers up to his shoulders. He watched the darkness until the sun rose.

He walked on the beach all morning. Something was going wrong. Had gone wrong. Why had he said all those things to Tara? It really hadn't mattered when she was alive. They *had* been happy. That was the reality. And now? Now he felt as though he were in some kind of nightmare.

He looked up and saw a woman walking toward him. *Julie.* This time he knew it wasn't Tara. She waved as she got closer.

"You look like you had the kind of night I did," she said when they met one another. Her eyes were red and puffy. "Melanie was up all night crying. She said someone kept whispering to her. I finally had to take her into bed with me."

"I'm so sorry, Julie," he said.

"It's not your fault," she said, laughing. Her laughter sounded forced, her voice tired.

Calder looked up at the sky.

"Isn't it a gorgeous day?" she said. "It's rare to find a November day so clear and warm."

He nodded.

"We could make a sand castle, or something," she said. "I feel like doing something silly."

"Why not? We'll do it until we freeze."

They sat on the damp sand and began digging. Julie laughed as she squeezed sand through her fingers. "Isn't this great?" Calder laughed, too. Julie was beautiful. Just as herself. She really looked nothing like Tara, except for her hair.

"You're staring again," she said. "Thinking of Tara?"

"No," he said. "I was thinking about you."

She smiled. "We need some water," she said, "and I've come prepared." She pulled a cup from her bag. "I'll get some." She ran toward the water, dusting sand from her slacks. He felt unexpectedly giddy as he watched her bend to scoop up the water. Happy.

Then she started walking into the water.

"Julie!" he called. "What are you doing?"

It was a bit cold for a swim. Besides, he had been told the undertow here was treacherous. Julie continued walking, awkwardly, the water now up to her knees. Waves were building near Table Rock. In a few seconds, they would break near shore and roll over her.

"Julie!" There was brine in the air, more pungent than the ocean smell. "Tara! What are you doing?" He stood and raced toward the water. Julie walked slowly, looking around confusedly. "Tara!" Calder called. "Let her go!"

He wasn't running anymore. He could hardly walk. The water was almost to Julie's waist.

"Julie!" he screamed. "Come back!" The wave broke, turned to foam, and Julie disappeared. "Tara, please let me go. You're killing her."

Julie's head came to the surface. She screamed his name.

Suddenly Calder was being propelled toward the water. A moment later, the cold water slapped over him. He held his breath and pushed himself to the surface, looking for Julie. Another wave was ready to break over his head. She was gone, all was silent except for the sea, and then Calder spotted her again. He called to her.

The ocean pulled at his feet. "Tara," he gasped. "It's me, Calder."

Tara watched their struggles become less frantic, more exhausted. The ocean would take them soon. They would no longer be able to touch one another. They would know what it was like to be as she was. Wandering the earth for eternity. Alone. She had not wanted to die. She had only wanted to save his life. It wasn't fair. They hadn't had enough time together. She loved him so much.

"Calder," she whispered, her voice an anguished part of the winds. She had loved him more than life itself. And now she was trying to kill him? This wasn't her. This wasn't what she wanted. How could she do this to him? How could she have done any of it? She wanted him to live. She whispered his name and then let him go. Saved him one more time. "Good-bye," she said.

The ocean pushed Calder to the surface. He choked and kicked to stay above the water. Julie was next to him. They pulled each other to the shore and collapsed on the sand. Wearily, they embraced. She slid onto his lap; he rocked her back and forth. Calder looked out at the water, and tears ran down his face. "Good-bye, sweetheart," he whispered.

"What happened?" Julie asked.

"Somebody just died," he said.

Cycles

They have a name for what is wrong with me, I am told. I say there isn't anything wrong with me that I'm not taking care of myself. Young people, especially women, often have this problem, my mother tells me. Later my grandmother tells me again.

It doesn't matter what they say to me; I won't eat. Or if I do, I go into the bathroom, lock the door and stick my finger down my throat. They don't realize I have to stop the thing from growing inside of me.

Six days a week, I work at the restaurant across the street from the restaurant where my mother works. It is not the fanciest part of town, nor is it the worst. It is only a twenty-minute walk from our apartment, and the whores, drunks, and junkies are at a minimum. My mother tells me I should be grateful we have jobs. My grandmother reminds me that her mother worked herself to death as a washerwoman. Often, my mother and grandmother seem to be the same person when they speak, only one is twenty years older than the other.

Once, I wandered into the university area and heard two women talking about their jobs. They were attractive college types, with wavy brown hair and cashmere sweaters.

"I like waitressing at the Pub," one of them said. "I meet so many interesting people!"

She seemed to bubble when she talked. I moved into the shade of an oak tree to listen unobserved. They were like two bright flowers in the sun.

"Yeah, I hear the theater people and some profs hang out there."

Someone came up to them then, and they walked away. Some days later I went by the Pub and stood outside. Inside, it was crowded and noisy and filled with well-dressed, laughing people. I saw pretty young things stuffing dollar bills into their pretty little aprons. It was no wonder the campus flower enjoyed her work. I get nickeled and dimed all day.

At home, it is all too obvious I don't eat. Grandma bends over her needlepoint (she sells it to a gift store downtown; they pay her minimum prices and then jack the retail price up five times or more) and urges me to have some dinner. She squints too much and coughs. When she turned thirty-five, she gave up smoking, but she still has the cough. She went to the doctor for it once and was told she needed to get out of the city. "Move?" she had asked. When the doctor said, "Yes, that would be best," she had laughed herself into another coughing fit. My mother quit smoking when she was thirty-five too. I never started. I suppose that is one way in which I differ from my mother.

It is not like I don't want to eat. I do. But I believe I am the only one who can stop this cycle, so I must do what I must do. I think about food all of the time. Every moment of the day I think about all the ways not to eat. Each morsel I reject is another victory for me: I am surrounded by eating people all day and still I don't take a bite. It gives me courage and strength. Perhaps I can conquer after all.

I realized early on that if I didn't eat at all, I'd die. And that is certainly not the point. The thing in me can die. Not me. So I eat a little bit when I deem it necessary. If I feel my body pulling at my muscles, eating them for energy, I go into the kitchen when everyone is asleep and nibble on something. Once, Grandma came in and I hid the food behind my back.

"Child, it is not a sin to eat," she said. "You pay for it. Eat it."

She does not understand. They both get angry with me.

"Just eat!" my mother said one day. I could tell she wanted to take a handful of food and cram it down my throat. "Just force yourself to eat!"

I stared at her. She started to cry.

"I suppose it is all my fault?" she said, sinking into the kitchen chair. It wobbled as she sat down. They are old, and we need new ones. "I've been reading about it. They say maybe you don't want to grow up. It seems kind of silly, since you're already eighteen years old. I just don't understand."

She left the room, and Grandma took her place, crying and shaking her head. Was it she who I would look like in forty years?

I think about what my mother said, about not wanting to grow up. It is one of the stupidest things I've ever heard. Who doesn't want to grow up unless it is some woman nearly forty years old like my mother who looks back at her life and realizes it was a waste? I want to grow up, to get away.

Sometimes I go out with Billy, one of our neighbors, but he becomes concerned about me, and he is too tired and old for his age. He talks about his sister and her husband who beats her, about his father and mother who drink too much. After a time I tire of him, too, and instead I spend my free time not eating or looking through the family album. Mostly the album is filled with pictures of Grandma, Mother, and myself. There are various relatives, but I don't know them anymore. A tall, handsome man with a beret is supposed to be my grandfather, but I don't believe it.

I grow weak at work. My boss tells me I should take some time off. He doesn't want to fire me, but he will soon, I know. It will kill me after all, won't it, if I lose my job?

I go to the library and study science magazines. I try to verify what I have suspected for some time. My grandmother had my mother when she was eighteen. My mother had me when she was eighteen. All three of us were born almost on the same date. I look at the photographs in the album and we are all the same, just different ages, living out the same life again and again. Sometimes I awaken at night, terrified, and it takes me a few seconds to realize this night terror is not mine but one my mother had when she was my age, or my grandmother.

My mother threatens to put me in a hospital, but we have no insurance, and she would never put me in a state hospital. She and Grandma take me to the neighborhood clinic. Because of my income, they say, I won't have to pay much. The doctor is rough and rude. He thinks he's God in his white uniform. He wants to know who I've been sleeping with. I stare at the wall and don't answer him. It is none of his business, but I haven't had sex with anyone in a long time. He would not, of course, believe in the virgin birth or spontaneous parthenogenesis, as the magazine article called it.

He shakes his head and says, "You people. Don't you know what contraceptives are? How are you going to pay for an abortion, or a baby, for that matter?"

I want to rip out his eyes, slice off his testicles, something that would be long drawn out and painful. What could he possibly know of my life, when he lives in the Heights and visits here once a week or once a month so he can feel superior?

Instead, I leave. It is too late. I have tried not feeding it. It didn't work. I don't think I understood, really, until now. Abortion is not even an option.

They ask me to leave my job. I am showing too much. My boss puts his arm across my shoulders as I cry. He promises I can have my job back afterward. Grandma and Mother tell me which agencies to go to for help. They have been through it before. I start smoking, just as

Grandma and Mother did when they were pregnant. I know it is not good for either of us, but I can't seem to help myself. At night I dream nightmares that are not my own. She is screaming already for me to let her out of her misery. I cannot, I cannot. I eat and sleep, and Mom and Grandma tell the neighbors I am better. I suppose it is more honorable to have a pregnant daughter than one who doesn't eat.

When I go into labor—I am early, just as my mother and grandmother were—I hear cries and feel pain that seem to be from someone other than myself, but someone who is myself. I wonder if either my grandmother or mother realized the truth. The baby comes out quietly. She is female, as I knew she would be, with a crown of black hair.

Suddenly she begins to cry. I cry too. Her tiny lungs pause for air and then she begins screaming in earnest. I open my mouth, and the sound I emit is identical to hers. The hospital staff in the room halt their routines and look at us. The screaming frightens the nurse, and she practically drops the baby on my stomach. I hold her tightly against me. I know the pain she feels. I have felt it for generations. Now she will feel it again. I hold her close and I am holding myself, my mother, my grandmother. The cycle will not end.

Someone else is crying now, someone who is not a part of us. I rock my baby against me, saying, "There, there." Her crying has stopped, and she lies quietly against my chest.

The doctor puts his fingers against my baby's neck.

"These people," he says, shaking his head, reminding me of the other doctor. He motions to the nurse, and she takes the baby from me. I feel tired and relieved. Perhaps it will be all right. Perhaps I am wrong, and the chain can be broken. "Life means so little to them," the doctor continues. "They don't know how to use contraceptives, constantly having children. Jesus." He slams his fist against the door and leaves the room. I hear the nurse sobbing; someone else is saying something about a broken neck.

My eyes widen and I call to them, asking for my baby, but she is gone. They all look over at me.

"Should we call the police or was it an accident?"

"Just let her alone," one says. "Can't you see she's half-crazy and half-starved? She probably didn't realize her own strength. The baby is dead. Let's just let the episode drop."

Dead? I bolt up and clutch my stomach.

"It's all right," one of the nurses says, touching my arm. "You're all right. It's over now."

Months later, I sit in our apartment in the wobbly chair, smoking and listening to Grandmother and Mother talk. I remember what the nurse said about it being all over, and I know now it will never end. I *am* different from my mother and grandmother. I touch my abdomen. Inside, I have begun all over again.

Sanctuary

I went back to the house yesterday. At first it seemed too different. The long twisting drive was almost overgrown. The lawn was covered with weeds; Kiri's flowers had all since died. Then I looked up at the pine trees swaying in the wind and heard the gentle noise of the sea air winding through them. My chest tightened and the memories came rushing back. I wondered, as I have wondered nearly every hour of my life for five years, how I could have done what I did to Kiri.

In the summer before my last year of college, I came to the tiny coastal town of Canyons to work in my uncle's store. I accepted his offer of work because I wanted to experience small town life. I had spent most of my life in cities and, as a future psychologist, I thought I should learn to deal with all kinds of people. And I needed a job.

My uncle's store served as a food, drug, and feed outlet for the town. Everyone knew my uncle Bob and within the week everyone knew me. First suspicions appeared to be instantly allayed when people were told: "This is Bob's nephew Jason." For the first week it seemed my entire name was "Bobsnephewjason."

Since I served as delivery person as well as stocker and cashier, I was able to see most of the town and some portions of the beach within the first week. I began to learn what home belonged to which people. Most of the houses were single-story frames, bent and crooked, as if shaped by the constant sea wind.

There was one house, however, that stood out among the others. I spotted it on a delivery run one afternoon. I stopped the car and looked up the drive. The house was built on a hill overlooking the beach and town. Tall evergreens shielded the wooden and stone two-story building from the winds. To one side of it was an enclosed greenhouse, and when I squinted, I could just make out a figure inside, bending over. Someone honked behind me, and I started up the car and left. Later I asked my uncle about it.

"That's the Marlin home. Kiri Marlin lives there."

"All by herself?"

"Yep," he answered, heaving a box of juice off the shelf and onto the dolly. I grabbed another and stacked it on top.

"Have I ever seen her in here?"

"No," he answered. "She doesn't leave her house."

"What?" I had visions of discovering a truly remarkable psychological case. I could study her, do a paper about her. I would become famous before graduating.

"I'd like to meet her," I said. "Does she see people?"

My uncle stopped bending and looked over at me. "Of course she sees people. I deliver her groceries once a week. She's just a lady who doesn't leave her house. Her parents were sort of eccentric, too."

"Actually, it isn't eccentricity. It's a condition called agoraphobia. It literally means an abnormal fear of open places. I didn't know it could run in families."

"She's not afraid of open places, Jason. She just doesn't leave her house. She used to, but she hasn't since her parents died."

"Why? How did they die?"

"They just died."

"Could I deliver the groceries next time she calls?" I asked.

He reluctantly agreed. "I'm only allowing this because you are a relative, not really an outsider. I'm trusting you not to bug her. We all like Kiri. She's part of this town and we don't want anything to happen to her."

"I'm not going to hurt her," I said. "I'm nice to old ladies."

Bob smiled. "Quit talking and get to work."

Two days later, Kiri Marlin called in her order. I helped get the requested items together and then I anxiously drove to her house. When I got out of the car, I noticed there wasn't any wind. I could hear it in the pine trees, a gentle whooshing sound I liked to listen to on nights just before a storm, but I could not feel it like I could in town—a damp wind that never seemed to stop. It was peaceful here, as if I had stepped into some kind of haven. I listened for a moment before reaching into the car for the groceries.

I rang the doorbell and a voice called for me to come in. I was mildly surprised that the door was not locked. I opened it and went inside. I expected cobwebs, darkness, perhaps a stale wedding cake or an old woman in a dingy wedding gown. Instead I was greeted by two cats, sunlight, bleached oak floors, vivid green ferns, and various hanging plants. The air was cool and fresh, as if a breeze were running through the house.

And then Kiri walked into the room, a totally different apparition from the one I had expected. She removed gardening gloves and held out her hand. I was struck dumb, but I managed to shake her hand.

"You must be Jason," she said, tucking the gloves into her jean pockets. "I'm Kiri Marlin." She smiled, and I guessed her age at around thirty. Light brown hair was pulled away from her face by two combs. Her pretty cheeks were flushed, as if she had been outside running.

She laughed. "Close your mouth, Jason. Emily Dickinson I'm not. Come on into the kitchen," she said, taking one of the bags from me.

I blushed and followed her into a large airy kitchen, where windows and plants outnumbered appliances and cupboards. One of her cats, a Siamese, leapt onto the counter and sniffed at the packages as I set them down.

"Are you enjoying your visit?" she asked as she began putting away the groceries.

"It's very different from where I come from," I answered.

"That doesn't answer my question," she said, "though I suppose it does in a way."

"Oh, I like it here, really, especially the ocean and the beaches."

"I like the ocean, too. Sunsets from here are spectacular," she said.

"You can see it from here?"

"Sure, I have quite a view," she said. "Come on, I'll show you."

She took me out of the kitchen and up a short flight of stairs into the living room. All of the west wall was made of glass. We were above the trees and had a panoramic view of the ocean. Today the water was dark green, flecked with white. A flock of birds flew over one of the shore rocks.

"It's nice, isn't it?" she said, smiling.

I nodded and turned from the window. I suddenly felt guilty for my earlier desire to examine her like some kind of specimen.

"Do you like games?" I asked, noticing several boxes on her bookshelves: a backgammon game, a go set, Scrabble.

"Yes, I guess I do."

"I've always wanted to learn go. Could you teach me?"

She turned and looked into my eyes for several seconds, as if she were trying to look deeper, to see into my soul.

"Sure, I'll teach you," she said. "You bring the pizza and be here at eight."

Kiri was a good and gentle teacher, but when I did something totally wrong, she reprimanded me, telling me I had not been listening. After nearly an hour in her company, I forgot she had this little quirk: She did not leave her house. We played and ate in the living room so we could watch the sun go down. As the evening passed, she asked me about school and my life, and I told her. She teased me when I told stories about parties I had attended in college.

"I don't want to hear about that," she said. "I want to know what you've learned. Not just at school, but in your lifetime."

"I'm not sure what I've learned," I said, "except how little I truly know." I was surprised at the things I could tell her—feelings and ideas I wasn't even aware of until I said them to her.

The cats each chose a lap and curled up to sleep.

"I've had Harlow, the Siamese, since my mother died," she said. She leaned against the couch and stroked the cat.

"When was that?" I asked.

"About eight years ago," she answered. "She's getting to be an old cat. I got Tori three years ago."

"How did your mother die?" I asked.

"Just like most people die," she answered. "She stopped living."

I remembered that my uncle hadn't told me how her parents had died, and I wondered what the big mystery was. I didn't pursue it, however, and the conversation moved away from her mother. We discussed books we had each read. I will remember that first evening always. Sometimes, now, I wish I could forget, or at least distort it so I don't remember how beautiful it was. That night, as always with Kiri, I was relaxed. There was no flirtation, no awkwardness between us. I just truly enjoyed the company of another person. The house creaked, the pines moved with the wind, and Kiri and I talked into the night.

Finally, when night was edging toward morning, I told Kiri I should leave. We cleaned the living room and then she walked me to the door. I hesitated, not wanting to go.

"May I come again?" I asked.

She looked into my eyes.

"You must know one thing, Jason," she said. "I do not leave this house. You must promise not to try to change that."

"I promise," I said, without thinking. She smiled. I would have promised anything that night just so I could see her again.

For the next week, I went over to Kiri's every night. Sometimes there were other people there, friends of hers. Some of them were people I had met in town or had seen roaming the beaches. They were nice, but I resented their presence. I wanted Kiri all to myself. She seemed to enjoy our time alone, too, showing me how she managed without leaving the house.

She was obviously proud of her greenhouse. It was filled with flowers and vegetables. I had never seen flowers so colorful or vegetables so lush, yet she used no fertilizers or other chemicals.

"Just my hands," she said.

I was not much of a gardener, but since Kiri enjoyed spending time in the greenhouse, I asked her to teach me how to be useful.

"I think teaching you to be useful would be a full-time job," she said, grinning.

I grabbed her. "I'll get you for that," I said. "I'll yell at your plants and give them neuroses."

She laughed, and I realized she was in my arms. My stomach seemed to twist inside itself. It still does when I think of that moment. I had never felt anything so wonderful—until I leaned over and kissed her. She put her arms around me, and we embraced.

She whispered my name and kissed me again.

"We're all dirty from the garden," she said. "I think we need a shower." She took my hand and we went upstairs.

I had never fallen so quickly and so much in love. We never ran out of things to say, yet often we just lay quietly in each other's arms, listening to the wind through the pines. One evening, we fell asleep on the couch together. I awakened to darkness; Kiri was gone. When my eyes adjusted to the dark, I could see Kiri by the window. I went and stood behind her. The moon was out, shining down on the beach and ocean. Two people walked along the tide mark. I put my arms around Kiri's waist.

"Do you wish you were down there?" I whispered.

"Good God, no," she answered, stiffening in my arms. "If all around you were flames and you were in the only safe spot, would you want to go into the flames?"

"Is that what it's like for you?" I asked. "Is it that frightening?"

"It is not so much frightening as . . ." She turned to me, searching for the right words. "As certain. I will die if I leave this house."

"But you will die inside this house someday, too," I said. "Think of all the things we could do together, places we could see before we die."

She covered my mouth with her hand. "Shh. You promised. You must accept me the way I am."

"Won't you even consider going for help?"

"Help? I don't need help, Jason." She pulled away from me.

I took her hand. "Can't you see it's not normal to be locked up in this house?"

She laughed, making it an almost unnatural sound. "Of course it's not normal. But it isn't just my psyche that's in danger, Jason. It's all of me." She sighed. "I've been out, and I'm nothing out there—insubstantial. Here, I'm something. I have control. Some people never find their niche in the world, I have. My parents tried to live outside this house. They failed. This is our spot. This is where I belong. I've accepted that. There is comfort in knowing where you belong, Jason.

"Kiri, I can help you if you let me," I said, as I took her face in my hands. "There is nothing outside this house that can't hurt you inside this house, too."

She stared at me, an unwavering look that made me think she was looking clear to my core. I dropped my hands.

"You can't understand," she said, "but you must accept that this is my place on Earth. End of discussion."

The conversation ended, but I continued to think about it. I needed to finish college. I couldn't do that in Canyons, but I didn't want to leave Kiri. I had always imagined myself traveling one day. I couldn't do that with Kiri, and I didn't want to go without her. I was so blind; if only I had realized how many places we saw together in her own home.

I was determined to cure her. I went to the library and found out what I could about agoraphobia. There wasn't much. They described physical reactions: perspiration, accelerated heartbeat, severe anxiety attacks. Therapists suggested gradually curing patients by taking them on small excursions outside the home.

One night I began looking through my uncle's library, hoping to find something to help me.

"Whatcha looking for, son?" Uncle Bob asked as he stood in the doorway.

"Psychology books."

He laughed. "Nothing but Zane Grey and Janet Dailey in this house," he said.

I smiled. I had never known anyone as well read as my uncle.

The house was packed with books. Bob came into the room and sat down.

"Let it be, Jason. What does it matter?"

"I want to do things with her," I said. "It hurts me to see her holed up in that house all the time."

"Why? Is she unhappy?"

"She says she isn't. But how could she be happy? It must feel like a prison."

"Or a sanctuary," he said. He leaned back in his chair. "She knows what's best for her, Jason. Her folks have been in this town, in that house, for generations. Made their fortune in the stock market, I believe. Before they died, Kiri's parents were important people in town." He squinted. "You know, I can hardly remember them anymore. It hasn't been that long since they died."

"How did they die?"

"Mr. Marlin was in a car accident," he said. "There were rumors he died before the car actually crashed into the ocean. There wasn't much left of him when they pulled the car out. It was the first time in decades he'd left the house. No one knew why he left. Some said Kiri's mother talked him into it." He shrugged. "Maybe it was a nice day and he wanted to go for a ride. Soon after his death, Kiri's mother walked into the ocean and drowned."

"So you think Kiri's fear comes from what happened to her parents when they left the house?"

"You aren't listening," he said. "Maybe she's got reasons to fear."

I shook my head. "There must be a way to help her, to free her from this fear. There must be."

Bob stood and stretched. "She doesn't have a problem with it, Jason. You do." He started to say something else, but instead, he left the room. I sat on the floor, wondering what to do next.

For weeks I worried about the end of the summer and the rest of our lives. Then suddenly I had the answer and I was elated—and afraid. Kiri never suspected what I was going to do—at least I thought so at the time. I chose a day that was particularly cool and breezy. The air moved nicely through the house, filling it with the smells of the outdoors. Clouds covered the sun, taking the summer brightness away. Kiri and I worked in the greenhouse. I helped her take flowers and put them in the wheelbarrow. Later I was going to plant them outside, around the living room windows.

"I get enough sunlight from the windows, but sometimes I think my flowers need to be outside," she said. Harlow bounded into the room like a kitten and jumped onto my shoulders. Tori pawed at my leg and meowed.

"They're hussies, aren't they?"

"Just like you," I said. I reached over and kissed her nose.

"How did you get off work today?" she asked.

"I asked for it off."

"That was clever," she said, laughing. Then she scowled when I tugged too hard on a root and it broke. "Patience, Jay. In any case, I'm glad you're here. I love these kinds of days." She whirled around. "I can't believe how happy I am!"

I caught her in mid-turn. The cat jumped away from me. "Happy! Well, I've got something that will make you even happier. Close your eyes."

"What?" She closed her eyes. "A surprise?"

"Yes." I tied a kerchief around her eyes and across her ears. Then I twirled her around a few times. I led her around the house, going up and down stairs, trying to disorient her. We both laughed. My heart began pounding too hard. I broke out in a sweat. I hoped I was doing the right thing, but I was afraid she would be angry with me. I stopped her for a moment and kissed her. She lifted her head up, blind, and grinned.

"I love you very much," I told her, suddenly frightened of what I was doing.

"I love you, too," she said. "Now take me to my surprise."

I twirled her one more time, led her in and out of two more rooms, and then I took her through the open front door. I talked and laughed so she wouldn't notice the change. I had even put some old boards on the sidewalk, hoping they would feel like her living room floor. I stopped her just out of the shadow of the house, about ten steps from the door.

"Jason, where am I? Can I see now?"

I slowly untied the kerchief. "See, you're safe," I said.

I will never forget the look on her face as she turned to me. It still troubles me at night: I open my eyes from a nightmare and I will see her face, inches from my own. Her eyes were opened wide in terror—and disappointment. I had betrayed her.

"You promised," she whispered.

Suddenly, it seemed that the sky was black. Or was it? I couldn't breathe or move. Perspiration rolled down my back. I became overwhelmed with anxiety. I was dizzy. I covered my eyes, trying to still the twirling world. What was happening to me? I reached for Kiri, but my arms flayed air.

Seconds later, I opened my eyes. The dizziness subsided. I looked around. It was a gorgeous summer day. The cats stood in the doorway watching me. A breeze moved through the pine trees.

And Kiri was gone.

I ran toward the house, calling her name. Inside, I wandered about almost blindly, bumping into doors and walls: I knew when I found her she would not ever want to see me again.

But I didn't find her. She wasn't in the house. I looked around the yard, too, but there was nothing.

And then I went to the greenhouse and found something near the windows. I'm not certain what—it looked as if some living thing had suddenly become unglued and melted into the ground, leaving behind its shadow like a kind of marker. I closed my eyes and quickly backed away.

They never found Kiri. For a time I was suspected of murdering her. The more I went over the events in my mind, the more I believed that to be true, but when I confessed, they didn't believe me.

Soon after, Kiri's recently made will was read. She declared that her substantial fortune and the house be left to me if she was not seen in the house for thirty days. When my uncle told me, I cried out, calling for someone to take away the pain. I realized then she had known all along I would not keep my promise.

The house stood empty until my return yesterday. The cats had fled long ago. I stood at the door trembling. I turned the handle. It was unlocked, as it had always been. I wanted to be sick as I opened the door. It all came rushing back, every second of the happiness we had shared in this house. And then I stepped inside. This time I found the cobwebs and darkness I had expected that first day. The house smelled of decay. I breathed the damp air deeply. I had done this. I was the cause. I looked around. The house was empty, as if Kiri had never existed.

I started to back away, to run out of the house, but something made me hesitate. Perhaps I could fix it up, make it alive again. I had traveled for five years, running toward anything that could make the memories go away even for a little while. Now I was weary of it. This was my home, my place in the world. I looked outside once more, and then I closed the door and shut away the light.

Sarah, Unbound

"Sarah, " Paul whispered, his breath warm on her ear. His lips brushed the small of her back and then kissed the tiny rose that bloomed from the dimple above her left buttock. "My tattooed lady," he said. She turned and drew him toward her, inside her. She saw stars in his eyes. "I will give you whatever you need," he whispered. Sarah gasped with pleasure.

Suddenly, she was eight years old. Her father's footsteps were quiet outside her bedroom door. Then he was in the room, pulling up her nightgown, groping for her in the darkness. He pushed the pillow over her mouth as he rammed himself into her.

The phone rang, and Sarah opened her eyes. Morning. She was alone. She sighed. The dream was all wrong. She didn't know a man named Paul and her father hadn't raped her until she was eleven. The phone rang again. She answered it.

"Sarah? It's Nancy. Did I wake you?" Her sister's voice did not sound two thousand miles away.

"Sarah?"

"No, I was awake," Sarah said. "What's going on?"

"Sarah . . ." Nancy's voice broke.

"What's happened?" Sarah's stomach was suddenly in a knot.

"It's Carl." Their brother. "He and Katie have split. Apparently he's been molesting his daughter."

The room shifted, slightly, and Sarah drifted. Who was that in the distance talking on the phone, her face white, her lips turning red where she bit them?

Sarah tasted blood, and she was on the phone again, listening to her sister cry. Molest. What a stupid word. He had *raped* his daughter. He had *assaulted* her. He had taken her body away from her.

"That bastard," Sarah said.

"Sarah!" her sister cried. "He needs our support." Easy for her to say. Their father never touched her.

"Like father, like son," Sarah said. There was silence on the other end of the phone.

Finally her sister said, "I'll talk to you later when you're calmer about all this."

Sarah set down the phone. When she got her degree a year ago, she had moved as far away from her family as she could —without leaving the country. It hadn't been far enough.

Suddenly she realized she did know someone named Paul. He came to her office once a week for counseling. Only he wasn't an adult. He was eight years old. Sarah grabbed her stomach. "My god," she whispered. She was having wet dreams about her young clients! "Like father, like son. Like daughter." She bit her lip until she tasted blood again.

Sarah's office seemed grayer than usual as April clouds covered Mount Hood in the distance and dropped down to become fog in the Columbia Gorge. She knelt onto the floor and pulled out the toy box. Sometimes children who had been molested became molesters. A learned behavior. Which meant she, too, could molest some innocent. She pulled out a black plastic horse from the box.

Paul loved this horse. She smiled. He called him Caesar. He was a mature child; only when they played together did he act like an eight-year-old. Sarah dropped the horse into the box. She felt too deeply for the children. She dreamed of them, and their wounds were open sores she could not heal. Children were too fragile; it was too easy to damage them permanently.

She closed her eyes. She heard her nightgown ripping, felt the pillow cover her mouth. How could her brother do what her father had done to her for countless nights?

Sarah pushed away the toy box and stood up and went to her desk. She thought about talking to Henry, the head of the counseling and resource center. She would ask to be taken off any cases which involved children. She knew what he would say. He would want to know if she had every touched or talked to her clients in a sexual manner. Of course she hadn't. Then he would remind her that dreams were only symbolic representations of other things. He would also tell her that she was very good with children. They seemed to instinctively trust her.

She rubbed her face and sighed. She had gone to counseling herself while completing her degree. They had talked about her childhood experiences with her father. She thought she had dealt with it all. So had the counselor. Now the memories were resurfacing. Like some kind of toxic waste.

She looked at her desk calendar. Paul was her first client this morning. He had been coming to her for two months, ever since his mother committed suicide by driving into the Columbia River as Paul watched. The mother had left behind a boy with little self-esteem. At each session, Sarah worked on making him feel important and loved. Later, she would help him feel anger. Today, they would play, as they often did. It was good for him to be a child for a little while each week.

Sarah went into the waiting room. Paul sat quietly, reading a *National Geographic* magazine. He was alone as usual.

His grandparents didn't think he should be coming to these sessions, but the court had insisted. He looked up and smiled when Sarah entered the room.

"Hello, Sarah, whose name is like a sigh," he said. His fine blond hair fell down across one blue eye. He put the magazine down and got up. Then he went to her and grasped her hand in his and said, "How are you today?"

"I'm good," she lied. "How are you?"

"Fine," he said.

They walked together into her office. Paul let go of her hand and went to the toy box. Sarah closed the door and then sat on the floor next to Paul.

"Caesar!" he cried, pulling out the horse. He laughed and galloped the horse across the carpet. Sarah took out another horse, a palomino with a purple saddle and golden mane and tail.

"I've been coming here for two months," he said. "I looked on the calendar. I like it here."

"I'm glad."

"It's safe here," he said. "Sarah, whose name is like a sigh, I'm going to marry you some day."

Sarah laughed. "Are you?"

He nodded. "And I'll give you whatever you need."

Sarah stiffened. The man in her dream had said that. Her heart raced: how had Paul known? No, no, he didn't know. He had probably said it to her before, and she had incorporated it into her dream. Yes, that was what had happened.

"And what do I need?" she asked.

He looked at her. "To be safe."

That was the second time he had mentioned being safe.

"What do you need?" she asked.

"I need to go away," he said. He rocked the horse back and forth.

"Why?"

"Because she told me to go away. She said she needed to be alone. Then she pushed me out of the car and drove into the river."

At last, he spoke of her death.

"Maybe that was what your mother needed. What do you need?"

He reached out and touched her hand lightly. Then he smiled.

"Are you going to leave me?" he asked.

"No, I'm not going to leave you."

He crawled up onto her lap, as he often did, and Sarah held him close. She rocked him gently and felt his tiny heart beating next to hers. His mother had killed herself, his father had left when Paul was three, after putting out a cigarette on his son's buttocks. Now Paul put his small arms around Sarah. He smelled clean and fresh, like Tide. Like the pillow her father had used to press against her mouth until she felt as though she was going to suffocate, and when she couldn't get her breath, she floated out of her body.

She went higher and higher until it seemed as though she was on the ceiling. Below, her father grunted, his pants down at his knees. She couldn't see herself beneath him. It was as though he was pushing himself into nothing. She floated to the stars and watched them twinkle. When she came back, her father was gone. She wiped up the blood and semen and wished she could go away forever.

Paul pulled away and looked up at Sarah. There were stars in his eyes. She smiled at him. She would not hurt him; she was sure of it. Not like she had been hurt. Not ever.

"There are stars in your eyes," she said.

"There are roses in yours," he answered.

"That's because you're seeing your reflection. And you're like a rose, a beautiful little flower!"

"Then that means you are a star," he said.

He kissed her cheek and then slid off her lap. They began playing with the horses again.

Sarah's mother called when she got home from work. She talked vaguely about Carl being in trouble.

"I know he's been raping his daughter," Sarah said, interrupting her mother.

"Sarah! That's nonsense. He's been accused of molesting his daughter. He's innocent until—"

"Until you can ignore it long enough to forget it?" Sarah said. She wanted to slam down the phone and be rid of her mother.

"You shouldn't dress that way," she had told Sarah once. "It only provokes men." Sarah had been thirteen and the loose, peach-colored dress was a birthday gift from an aunt. Sarah had hugged herself. She knew her mother was talking about provoking her father.

"You shouldn't be so angry," her mother said now. "You'll die an old bitter woman."

"Good-bye, Mother," Sarah said. She dropped the phone into its cradle. Why did her mother bother to call? She had never admitted that her husband had raped her daughter on a regular basis, even after Sarah told a school counselor when she was sixteen. When confronted, her father had denied it, and her mother refused to discuss it. She stayed with Sarah's father, and he stopped coming to Sarah's bedroom. But that was it.

Sarah unplugged the phone and went to the bathroom and took off her clothes. The day had seemed endless. Paul was the only bright spot. She had been nauseated all day, like she had been when she was eight and her father first came into her room and roughly fondled her. After that, she had always felt nauseated, until she was nineteen. She was in her second year of college when she found a tattoo place and had an illustrated man scratch a rose tattoo in her dimple. Her way of reclaiming her body.

She twisted her neck to look at the tattoo. It was a tiny blossom, barely visible. She had been proud of it; now she wanted to cover it up. She didn't want to think of her body and what her father had done to it.

She stepped into the shower and turned on the water. She closed her eyes and thought of Paul. Today he had spoken of his mother's death. Maybe soon he would cry. He needed to. She wished she would cry. She hadn't since she was eight years old.

That night, Sarah dreamed she stood at one end of the Hood River Bridge. The Columbia River flowed beneath her. She was wrapped in gauze like a modern day mummy. On the other side, Paul stood, his child's arms held out to her. Between them was darkness. Sarah couldn't move. She couldn't breathe.

She woke up gasping for air. She lay still for several minutes until her heartbeat went back to normal. Then she wrapped the blanket tightly around her. She was frightened and alone, a child again with no safe place left in the world. She hoped morning would come quickly.

She felt tired and lost at work the next day. She told the secretary that she wasn't in if anyone related to her called. The secretary laughed and said she understood.

Sarah went into her office and closed the door. She wished she understood. She should have dealt with all of this by now. She had moved to the West Coast to get away from her family and the memories, yet here they all were again. When she was younger, she had thought the only way to escape it all was by dying. But she didn't want to die, so she had just gone away. She had floated above it all. A living ghost. She couldn't stop her father, but she didn't have to participate. She left and wished she never had to return to her damaged little body. Sometimes, she felt as though she had never really completely returned.

Sarah stayed in the office long after everyone had left. Near nine, she went outside to eat a sandwich. She sat on the steps and turned her back to the lights of Hood River and stared up at the stars.

"Hello, Sarah, whose name is like a sigh."

"Paul," Sarah said. "Where did you come from? Isn't it late for you to be out?" He sat next to her on the steps.

"I was watching the stars. I followed one and it led me here." He smiled. "Tomorrow's Saturday, so I can stay up late."

"Do your grandparents know you're gone?" Sarah asked.

He shook his head. "They're asleep."

They were drunk, Sarah supposed.

"Look, there's the Big Dipper," he said, pointing to the sky.

"And there's the little one," she said.

Paul laughed. "You and me."

"Two dips?" Sarah said.

"Two dippers! You're silly!"

She laughed. They watched the stars for a time.

"How are your grandparents? Do you like living with them?"

He shrugged. "They don't notice me much. I go away sometimes."

"What do you mean?" Sarah held out half of the sandwich to him. He took it.

"Sometimes, when my mother was screaming or my father was around, I'd go away. You've done it before. I remember."

"What are you talking about?" she asked. He had never spoken of this before.

"I float away. I did it the first time when my father put out his cigarette on me. Called me an ashtray. Grandpa says I was too young to remember, but I do. I was three. I floated away to the stars. I met them all. They were my friends. You were up there, too. You breathed your name like a sigh."

Sarah remembered one night when her father raped her, one of the last times, nearly six years ago; she had left her body and floated above the house, the street, the town. For a moment, she had sensed other souls pressing up against hers. Now she looked at Paul and wondered if those souls had been other abandoned or abused children trying to find a safe place in the world.

He smiled. "You were a rose blooming across the sky," he said. He looked at his feet. "My grandparents say I can't come here any more."

"Here to see me?" Sarah asked.

He nodded.

"Do you want to keep coming?"

He looked surprised. "Yes. I like playing together. I can teach you all about the stars, and you can teach me about playing horses."

"You are a wonderful child," Sarah said. She rubbed the top of his head. "Don't worry about your grandparents. I'll talk to them. It'll be all right."

"I better go now," he said. He started down the drive and then he stopped and looked at her. "I'm glad you came down out of the stars. I like you here."

She watched him disappear into the darkness. She stood until she saw him under a street light again, and then she watched until he reached his grandparents' house. She finished her sandwich, and then she went home.

Sarah dreamed about Paul. This time, they walked across the bridge together, hand in hand. Whenever the darkness started to close in around them, they laughed at it and it drifted away like smoke. The sky was filled with stars which blossomed into white roses.

Sarah drove to her office first thing the next morning. She sat in the middle of the floor and pulled the toys from the toy box. She galloped Caesar and the palomino across the carpet and laughed. This was why she enjoyed her sessions with Paul so much. She was a child during their fifty minutes. They were growing up together. Her only real childhood.

She pushed the toys away and looked around. She shuddered. She felt afraid so much of the time. Like the darkness was just around the corner waiting for her. A darkness her father had brought into her life when she was eight.

Sarah stood and got a piece of construction paper and a box of crayons from her desk. She often had the children draw, another way to express themselves. She pulled out a brown crayon. At first, it felt fat and awkward in her fingers as she drew an outline of a man. Then she wrote "Daddy" across his torso. She picked up the blunted children's scissors and cut out the figure. She took a matchbook from a candle holder on her desk and then went to the bathroom. She lit a match and held Daddy's foot to the flame until it caught. The fire ate his feet. The pillow pressed harder against her face. She gasped for air. She was thirteen, and she put her hand between her legs and gently rubbed the place where it hurt. The fire licked her father's crotch. He was always so hard and hurtful, disgusting as his penis rammed up against her. She was too tiny. The flames ate his buttocks and started up his back. Sarah began to cry. And always as he pushed into her he whispered that he loved her, loved her, loved her. His body spammed and shuddered, and he did not see her. The fire severed his body from his head. The ashes floated into the sink. Sarah choked on her sobs. Then she screamed. She hated him so much. She had loved him. Why had he done it? The fire ate his mouth, his eyes. Sarah's scream became a wail. She dropped the last bit of paper into the sink before the flames touched her fingers. "Good-bye." she whispered.

She wiped her tears and turned on the water and washed the ashes down the drain. There went her father. Her brother. Her mother. All the bad memories. She looked around. Everything appeared fresh and new, as if all had been out of focus and now it was clear and sharp. Perhaps all these years, parts of her had been scattered across the universe. Now she had come home to her body. Or almost. It would take time. But she was safe. She was whole again. Now she was ready to protect herself and Paul. She would make certain he was safe and happy.

She turned off the water, went to the front door, and opened it. The darkness was gone. She thought of the stars in Paul's eyes, and she smiled and stepped out into the morning.

An Awful Leisure

I saw Stephen at the dance hall on the bluff several months after I died. He stood amongst the ruins, facing the ocean and the setting sun. He was still, his face like marble. The sun washed across him first gold and then rose, and he looked like something Michelangelo would have sculpted, only more human, more beautiful with his flaws. He closed his eyes, and his face softened with pain.

I wanted to run to him, to touch him. He was a living being. His life pulsed around him in blue and white waves. He looked older than the boy who had tagged along with me and my banal friends as we went from coffee shop to coffee shop talking of art.

"Stephen," I whispered, knowing he could not hear me.

He turned unexpectedly and saw me. I was stunned into stillness. His eyes opened wide in terror and madness. I smiled in the hope that I could ease his mind.

He held out his hands to me and then began screaming and shaking his head. I wanted to hear his screams: I knew he was calling my name.

He disappeared with the sun.

"You know him, don't you?" Janet drifted to the dance hall. She was smiling. She always smiled. She told me she smiled even as she drew the blade across her wrist. She was odder than all the rest, though not nearly as odd as I was. Even in death, I was the outsider.

"He was a friend," I said. I moved closer to her. She drifted away to the grass near the crumbling steps of the dance hall.

"That was cruel," she said, laughing, "letting him see you. You should have hid. I saw his face, Vanessa. He was in love with you."

I watched the waves crash against the rocks scattered along the shoreline. Stephen in love with me? The boy who half-carried me up five flights of stairs to my apartment after countless endless nights of too much alcohol? The boy who listened to me dissect old lovers while he fed me lasagna or spaghetti or anything starchy and fattening; he believed I drank too much and ate too little. I thought of him standing on the bluff screaming my name, and I realized he was no longer a boy.

"Do you suppose they ever got the blood out of the carpet?" Janet was at my ear, smiling.

My fingers ached; I wanted to touch something real. I grabbed Janet's arm. Her skin was warm, her flesh solid. She hissed.

"Please," I pleaded, "I need to feel something."

"You should have thought of that before you killed yourself." She laughed and stuck out her tongue at me.

I released her arm, and she disappeared. I sat on the steps. I could not feel the steps or the wind I saw pushing against the trees. I could not smell the salt air. I could not feel anything except the others, and they would not let me touch them. I put my head in my hands.

Maybe Stephen would return tomorrow. It was rare when we saw one of the living, and even rarer for one of them to see us. Still, I hoped.

I passed a restless night, floating from one place to another. The others scattered when I came near. They only got together to discuss their suicides, like old farmers talking about a good harvest. Janet waved and whispered, "I bet they never got out the stain," before drifting away again.

Morning came. I stayed in the dance hall and watched. Near sunset, Stephen appeared on the dance hall steps. His eyes and face were red. I moved slowly toward him. He looked up and stared. All the pain and love was so apparent in his face; I must have been blind or stupid not to have seen it before.

He said something. I shook my head and pointed to my ears. He pulled a piece of paper and pencil from his shirt pocket and wrote on the paper. Then he held it out to me. I read: Vanessa? Is that really you?

I nodded. He held out the pencil to me. I shook my head again. He shrugged, not understanding. I reached for the pencil. My fingers went through it. He nodded. Then he snapped his fingers and signed to me.

I laughed. Several years earlier, Stephen had taught me sign language. He had wanted me to get a job as an art teacher at a school where he taught hearing impaired children. That was when I first started having trouble selling my sculptures.

"It'll be something to fall back on," he told me, "until your pieces start selling again."

I picked up signing easily, as I did most languages. I drank too many glasses of white wine before the interview, however, and my prospective employers were not amused by my semi-pornographic joke—even though I signed it to them.

"I've been looking for you," Stephen signed to me now on the dance hall steps.

"Pardon me? Don't you know I'm dead?" I signed, trying to make a joke. I smiled.

He looked grim. "Of course I know you're dead. I found you— and you'd been dead for quite a few hours." His face contorted as he remembered. I wished I could touch him. He had always been a physical person. He let me hug him, sit on his lap at parties, walk hand in hand with him down the street. He was young; I had thought it all harmless fun.

"Why did you do it?" he signed, brushing away a tear. His green eyes were beginning to look slightly mad.

"I was tired," I signed. "I really don't know why. Stephen, Stephen." I signed his name several times, trying to get his attention as his eyes became bright with water. He had always seemed so in control. Perhaps I had startled him into insanity.

"Stephen, you are not crazy. I am really here. Please, stay with me, talk. Look at it this way: I'm sober."

His hands were still. I sat near him, hoping I could feel some of his life. He reached for me, and his fingers moved through mine, as if through air or some thing which does not exist.

"How's life?" I asked.

"Not the same without you," he signed. "Thanks for willing me the sculptures."

"You're welcome. I hope you threw them out. They were truly hideous."

"They were beautiful," he said. "They are in my apartment. I feel closer to you with them."

We were quiet for a time, watching the ocean together.

"I'm sorry you found me," I said. "I'm sure that wasn't pleasant."

"I didn't get your message for almost a day," he signed. "My roommate forgot to tell me you called. Otherwise I would have been there sooner. I would have saved you."

"Stephen, I came to this one-horse town so that no one would find me. That was the whole idea."

He turned to look at me. "Then why did you leave me a message?"

"I don't know! Can't we forget about it? It's all in the past."

As I looked into his eyes, I knew that was not true. He smiled wanly, and then he disappeared.

"Stephen!" I cried, hurrying from one corner of the ruined dance hall to another."

Janet appeared and stood watching me. "He'll be back," she said. "Can't you see. He's almost one of us."

"Don't say that, you wretch!" I screamed. The scream became a hideous wail. I closed my mouth.

Janet smiled. "Come, let's wander and you can tell me all about your death. You've never shared that juicy little tidbit, you realize."

"Of course I realize!" I stopped close to her face. She did not move. "I'm not like all of you, wallowing in the terrible wonder of my death, like pigs in slop, all of you! It's a mistake. I don't belong here."

"You did kill yourself, didn't you?" she asked. I said nothing. "Then you belong here—even if you don't act like the rest of us. You're odd but not unheard of. Come."

I sighed deeply. Stephen was gone for now, so I followed Janet. As it grew dark, we wandered about the empty town, passing through the ruined buildings easily.

I stopped at the motel where I had stayed the night I killed myself. The unlit neon sign hung from one nail, ready to fall. The doors and windows were all open. Several walls had caved in. I wondered how many people were living in the hotel now—even in the room where I lay dying only a few months ago. They were seeing a different reality than I was. I hoped Stephen was not staying in this motel

"This is the place you died," Janet said. "I can tell by the devastation. Very complete. Did you ruin many lives when you died?" She turned to me, smiling. I wanted to hit her.

"No," I said, my voice shaking. "I didn't ruin anyone's life, except possibly my own."

I left Janet staring at the motel, imagining my death.

I was a guest lecturer at Stephen's college when I first met him. He came up to me after class and said he admired my work. I invited him out for lunch. I drank tonic water. Stephen picked at his salad, shy and nervous. His innocence was charming. After that lunch, Stephen was a constant part of my life.

I was on my best behavior for the first few months of our friendship. Then I broke up with one of my lovers. I can't remember his name. I had one glass of wine and then another, until an entire bottle was gone. I didn't stop until I was throwing up in my bathroom with Stephen holding my hair away from my face. Later he took off my clothes and put me into a cool bath and sponged me off.

"You're not supposed to do this for drunks," I told him as I sat in the bathtub crying. "We're supposed to wake up in our own vomit. That way we'll cure ourselves."

"You're not a drunk," he whispered, kissing the top of my head. "You're Vanessa."

Now, I looked around my ruined world as the sun started coming up. I had been stupid for years. Stephen had been right there waiting for me all the time. And I'd never even noticed.

Before sunset, I found Stephen walking about the ruins. He was there earlier than he had been yesterday. I waved to him. He smiled. He looked better—no longer a man going mad. I wanted to run into his arms. Then I remembered we could not touch.

"I'm so glad I found you again," he signed. I smiled. "Let's walk along the beach for a while, all right?" His smile was desperate. He was going to pretend we were two ordinary people out for a walk.

"All right," I signed. I would pretend, too.

Stephen walked in front of me as we descended the bluff to the beach. Watching his back was comforting. It was familiar, safe. Watching him made it easy to imagine for a while that we were a normal couple.

Stephen slipped off his shoes and walked in the water. I drifted next to him and wished I could feel the icy Pacific, too. The sun was out. Clouds were building on the horizon. In a couple of hours, the fog would roll in.

"What's it like where you are?" Stephen asked.

I shrugged. "You see a thriving little tourist town. I don't. I see a world in ruin."

"Are you alone?"

I shook my head. "There are others like me."

"Like you?"

"Others who have killed themselves right in this little town." I thought of my naked dead body, Stephen's last look at me. Had I become hard after I died? Did I bloat up? Turn purple?

"Vanessa, I've moved here. I quit my job and I'm going to find one here," Stephen signed hurriedly. I stared at him. His aura seemed to reach out to me. I wanted to be closer. "We can be together," he signed.

"How?" I asked. "I never know when or if you'll return."

"We'll figure it out," he signed. "I already know we see each other around sunset—that's when you died. And each day, I see you earlier and for longer periods of time." His eyes were gentle, sad. "I can't lose you again," he signed. "You don't know what it was like to find you. To be without you. You must have known that I loved you."

I reached out to touch his cheek. I stopped and put my hands behind my back. We started walking again.

"When did you realize you loved me?" I asked.

He smiled. "After that first sponge bath. You let me see you that night."

"I was naked!"

He laughed. "I don't mean that. You really let me see your soul."

A cloud covered the sun, and the beach became gray. Stephen and I moved off the tide mark and up to the dry sand. He sat in the sand, and I sat facing him.

"When you were drunk you saw me," he signed. He stared off to sea. His hands were still for a moment, and then they moved slowly, deliberately, as if he was not quite certain what to say. "I know it's selfish, but I didn't mind it when you were drunk. You told me you loved me when you were drunk. In the morning, you never remembered."

I still didn't remember.

"When you were drunk, I believe you did love me," he signed. "You touched me. You let me near."

That was true. I craved bodily contact when I was drunk. It soothed the terror in my soul. Stephen always gave me the contact—without demand.

I shook my head. How could I have gone from one stupid lover to the next trying to find someone to make the nights easier when Stephen had been there all along?

Perhaps that was what had frightened me: always unable to find or accept goodness in my life.

I started to cry. Stephen signed, "What's wrong? Are you all right?"

He faded and then disappeared. I moved quickly to the spot where he had been and felt his aura. For a moment, our hearts beat together.

I drifted back up to the dance hall, terrified I would never see Stephen again. Janet sat on the steps humming. The beach was almost dark now.

"What's wrong with you? You look strange," Janet said. She smiled and continued humming.

I was cold. I rubbed my arms quickly. My fingers ached. I

felt stupid. *I was in love with Stephen.* And I had to die in order to realize it? Stupid!

"Janet, don't you ever feel anything?" I asked. "Don't you ever want to hold someone in your arms again?"

"Don't be disgusting," she said. "No! None of us does. It's easier to be alone. Why are you so peculiar?" She smiled, moaned, and then disappeared.

I wandered about the town for hours. The sun rose. I felt panicky. What if I never saw Stephen again? Even if I did, what good would it do? We could not really be together.

Near dusk I sat on the steps of the dance hall. Stephen did not appear. My fingers throbbed. I wanted to touch something. Clay? Even if I was still able to feel clay, I wasn't sure I could still sculpt. In the last years of my life, my works had become misshapen, grotesque. One critic said my pieces looked like things out of a drunken nightmare. If she had only know how close she had come to the truth.

Her article was published soon after my last lover left me: after calling me a drunken bitch. He would know; we were one and the same. I had tried to find Stephen that day, but he was out of town. I decided to leave town, too. Perhaps away from every-thing I knew I could stop thinking. Stop drinking. I called Stephen and told his roommate where I would be. Then I drove to a little coastal town Stephen and I had talked about visiting.

The ocean made me sad. The rain made me crazy. The wine made it all worse. I knew Stephen would be there any moment. Any second. I took the pills because I had to sleep. I had to stop the craziness. I had to end the ache I could never explain. No one ever understood it. Not even Stephen. It was a constant ache, a reminder that nothing was ever going to be right.

Then I was here, dead, with no one to touch.

"Stephen," I whispered. He could not be gone now. I had only just found him! I drifted to the motel where I had last been alive.

It was dark and eerie. I went down the deserted hall to my room. Inside, the room was empty except for a double bed.

I moved closer. Stephen slept in that bed. Moonlight came through the roof and lit his face. He looked like a boy again.

I lay on the bed beside him. He turned in his sleep to face me. Slowly his eyes opened. For a moment, I thought a miracle had happened. I was not truly dead. It had all been a dream. He smiled at me. His hand reached for my face. Yes, yes, I would feel his skin against mine. I would smell his smell. We would make love until the morning. His hand went through my cheek and onto the pillow. I screamed and jumped off the bed. Stephen sat up quickly and pressed his back against the wall.

We stared at one another for a long time.

"What are you doing here?" I signed. "I waited at the dance hall."

"I asked the manger if I could see your room," he answered, "for just a minute. I wanted to try and make sense out of what is happening. I sat on the bed, I guess, and fell asleep. I was exhausted. I hadn't slept since I first saw you on the bluff." His chin dropped to his chest and his shoulders shook. Surely this was hell.

"I can't live without you," he signed, looking at me again.

"Stephen, I do love you. I'm saying it now, and I'm not drunk. I want to make love with you. I want to be with you."

"Vanessa." His lips moved as he signed my name.

"I can't come back to your world," I said. "I wish I could. If you died in this motel room right now, perhaps you could come to me." I stopped. I could not believe I had signed those words.

"If I was dead, I still couldn't touch you. We'd still be apart," he said.

I shook my head. He got out of bed.

"What do you mean?" he signed. "You can touch the others?"

I should say no, I told myself. Tell him I could not touch anything ever. I loved him. I couldn't ask him to die, yet I could not bear being alone any longer. I wanted him. If he killed himself, he might come here, to me. Then we would have each other for an eternity.

"I can touch the others," I finally signed.

He moved closer. "Then that's out answer, isn't it?"

I started to sign no. To tell him that he could not do this thing. But I didn't. I nodded. Then he faded and was gone.

I screamed.

I had just told the man I loved to kill himself.

Janet came into the room. She smiled. "Nice boy."

"Leave me alone," I said.

"I thought you hated that," Janet said. "You sent him off to die, didn't you?"

"I would have stopped him, but he left! He won't really do it. He can't."

I paced the room. Holes appeared in the sheets; the mattress sagged in the middle. I did not really want Stephen to die.

"I thought you said you didn't ruin anyone's life when you killed yourself," Janet said. She drifted through a wall and vanished.

"I didn't mean it," I said. "Don't die."

I sighed and stared up through the gaping roof at the stars. I had meant it.

Trembling, I went to the dance hall and waited.

At sunrise, Stephen picked his way through the ruins. The blue and white aura was gone. He was dead.

I cried his name and ran toward him. It didn't matter now that I had suggested he died. We would soon be together forever. He looked up and waved.

Moments later, I was in his arms. He smelled slightly sweaty from walking. His skin was warm, textured. His heart pounded next to mine. This was ecstasy!

"Stephen," I whispered.

He took my arms and gently pulled away to look at my face.

"Stephen?"

"I thought it would all come back when I saw you," he said.

"What? I don't understand."

"Vanessa, I don't feel anything any more. My love for you—everything—it's gone." His eyes were empty. He looked like the others.

I moaned. The moan turned into a wail. What had I done?

"I am sorry," he said. "I'd like to be alone now."

I stepped back. Stephen walked away from the dance hall. I watched until I could no longer see him. Then I turned and looked down at the ocean. I wished I could jump and end it all.

I could not. I flexed my fingers. They ached worse than ever.

"Stephen," I whispered.

I turned away from the sea to begin the awful leisure.

Occupant

Peter stopped unpacking for a moment to gaze down at Greystone Bay. The line where the ocean and the town met was blurred, as if the foundations of the dark New England homes were made from seawater. The morning fog shifted to the east as he watched, and the town appeared to move slightly, draping itself around the bay like some scaly prehistoric creature.

Peter turned from the window and took his typewriter out of its case. He placed it on the table near the window and then ran his fingers across the keyboard. Here in the Bay, he would finally be able to write uninterrupted. He wouldn't be bothered by Mary or the phone or his former colleagues at the newspaper. He had left all that three thousand miles away.

As he glanced out the window again, he felt a rush of freedom. The fog had burned off and now the sun was out. He wanted to explore. He practically skipped outside and looked up and down the street. The other homes on his block were close together, yet each of the two- and three-story houses seemed like fortresses, with curtains drawn and gates closed. Steam rose from huge empty stone porches. His rented house looked puny in comparison.

He stepped through his wrought-iron gate and swung it closed behind him. The hinges creaked loudly in the silence and he glanced about uncomfortably, feeling as he had as a child when he made too much noise in the library. He grinned and went to the row of mailboxes at the curb. He shouldn't complain; he wanted a place where neighbors stayed to themselves, and had spent a week in a rented car driving up and down the coast looking for a town like Greystone Bay—one with few civic organizations or tourist attractions.

As he opened his mailbox and looked inside, he heard the echoes of children laughing. He closed the empty box and quickly walked down the deserted street toward town.

On the waterfront, Peter went into a diner with few people inside. An older woman dressed in a pink uniform came from behind the counter and held out a menu to him.

"No, thank you," he said, sliding into a booth next to the window. "I'd just like some coffee with honey, please."

"Honey?" she said. "I'm not sure we have any. I'll check in the back."

A minute later she returned with coffee and a tiny plastic bear filled with honey.

"Thank you," Peter said.

The waitress nodded and walked away. He was grateful she wasn't the talky type. He wanted to get to know the locals eventually, but for now he didn't want any distracting relationships.

Peter sighed pleasurably and leaned back in his chair. He had dreamed of living in a place near the ocean where he could spend all of his time writing. Now he had found it. He looked at the men who sat at the counter drinking coffee and talking quietly among themselves. Their faces were dark and lined, as if they had each spent a lifetime running against the wind. He wondered if any of them had pursued their dreams. He took a newspaper from the stack on the jukebox behind his table and opened it up. It was a typical small-town paper, he decided as he scanned the pages, filled with tacky local ads and gossipy news items. His dream fifteen years ago had been to work on a newspaper and win a Pulitzer. Things—people—always seemed to be in his way. Now all that had changed.

He sipped his coffee and gazed out at the bay. He was certain he was going to like this town.

Later in the morning, Peter found a grocery store within walking distance of his house. At the checkout he asked the clerk, "Is the weather always like this?"

The man nodded blankly and handed him his change.

"Thanks," Peter said, picking up his bag. "Nice talking with you."

Once home, he sat at the typewriter and stared out at the ocean. Several fishing trawlers were coming into the bay; some moved sideways as they fought the wind and waves. Mary liked fishing, he remembered. She had tried to get him to go with her on several occasions. "You don't have to fish," she would say. "Just keep me company." He never went.

He tapped his typewriter keys and shrugged her memory away. Mary was a part of the past now, too.

Peter prepared several manuscripts to send out. As he put them in the mailbox, the mailman drove up. He let his truck idle while he whistled tunelessly and opened boxes.

"Any mail for me? Peter Gibson?" Peter asked.

The mailman looked up, squinted, and glanced at the house. "Nope," he said.

"That's funny," Peter said. "I thought some of my mail would have been forwarded by now. I left a week ago."

"Sometimes that takes a while," the mailman said, reaching into Peter's mailbox and taking out his manuscripts. He put the flag down and started the truck forward again.

Peter watched him drive away. He should have heard from at least one of the editors by now. Several of his stories had been out for months. He shrugged. No news was better than rejection slips, he supposed, and looked up and down the street. It was Saturday afternoon, yet no one was outside washing a car or playing ball or screaming at children to behave. Nothing except silence. He walked toward the house. Perhaps it was the fog. Who would want to wash a car or play ball in the fog?

That night he dreamed of Mary. When he awakened to the sound of wind blowing against the house, he couldn't remember much, only that Mary had stood at his door knocking soundlessly. Peter got out of bed and padded into the darkened living room.

Outside, the trees looked like bloated figures bending to the harvest. Grey clouds skirted the full face of the moon. Where moonlight shone on the bay, Peter glimpsed ships with canvas sails inflated by the wind. An instant later, clouds covered the moon and the ships disappeared.

Peter sat at his desk and watched the black trees sway back and forth. Why had he dreamed of Mary? Although he left her a week ago, he had stopped loving her long before. Mary had known something was wrong, but when she suggested counseling a year ago, he refused. Instead he sat at his typewriter knocking out short stories between assignments at the newspaper, biding his time and waiting for the right moment to change his life. The night he left, Mary sat on the bed crying quietly while she watched him pack.

"You never even tried," she told him. "You never even put your name on the mailbox."

"I didn't promise to stay," he said.

Poor Mary. He had not meant to hurt her, really; he had just— forgotten her.

He looked out his front window. Several windows in his neighbors' houses glowed golden, as if lit from the inside by candles. Perhaps the electricity had gone out because of the storm. He turned on the desk lamp. The darkness seemed solid. Only his typewriter was illuminated. He switched on the machine. As long as he could see to type, he had all the light he needed.

A week passed and still Peter received no mail. When he went to the post office and questioned the postmaster, the man smiled and shrugged. "These things happen," he said. Peter wrote to his former post office in California to make certain they had his correct change of address.

He spent most of his time writing. Sometimes he walked to the wharf restaurant and had lunch. The same waitress always served him. Each day she treated him as though she had never seen him before. The clerk at the store was the same way. Peter told himself they needed time to warm up to him. It was a small town, after all, and he was a stranger.

At the end of the week, he put out another manuscript. The mail truck pulled up.

"Good day," the mailman said.

Peter grinned, glad the man had noticed him.

"Any mail for me today?" Peter asked.

The mailman squinted and looked out at the ocean. The horizon was covered with clouds.

"Damn fog," the mailman said. He opened Peter's box and took out his manuscript. "No mail for you," he finally said.

"I can't understand it," Peter said. "Isn't there at least something addressed to 'occupant'?" He smiled.

"Nope," the mailman said. The truck jerked forward.

Peter went into his house and tried to think of someone to whom he could write. If he sent letters, perhaps someone would answer them. He typed notes to his former editor and one of the reporters at the paper. He hadn't written to either of his brothers, Dave and Mark, for years. They spoke on the phone occasionally during the holidays, but that was it. After his parents died ten years earlier, he lost touch with them. Now he felt awkward typing out letters to them. What could he say? He knew so little about their lives.

Some time later, he sealed the letters and went outside in the dark to put them in the mailbox. He paused before going inside again. The fog made the streetlights glow unnaturally. Everything was indistinct; lines wavered. He could barely tell where his neighbors' houses began and the darkness ended. He put the flag up. He hoped someone would write soon.

When Peter awakened the next morning, he felt edgy. He sat at his typewriter and wrote as usual, but he couldn't concentrate. He watched for the mail truck. After it came and left, he ran outside, opened the box, and put his hand inside. It was empty. Why wasn't there an advertisement at least? What about his magazine subscriptions? Didn't he owe someone money somewhere? He went back to his typewriter and wrote to his magazine editors, his banks, old school friends. Someone would have to answer.

Several days passed and still there was no mail. Whenever Peter left his house, he felt eyes watching him through curtained windows. He wondered if they waited until he was away to come out of their homes. Downtown Greystone Bay moved about like any other town, except Peter felt like he wasn't there. The stupid waitress still had to be asked to bring honey for his coffee. And the clerk called him Mr. Morgan or Mr. Jones, even after he had taken a check from Peter and looked right at his name.

The fog was everywhere, clinging to Peter like a damp shirt. Sometimes it cleared, and he went down to the bay and walked along the tidemark. Even the gulls appeared indifferent, hardly acknowledging him when he tossed stones at them.

One afternoon he went to the post office.

"What is happening with my mail? I can't believe it could take this long to get to me," he told the postmaster.

The man smiled at him. "Mr. Gibbons—"

"Gibson!" Peter cried. "How can you expect to get my mail to me when you can't even remember my name!"

"Mr. Gibson, I assure you, if you were getting any mail we would deliver it," the man said. "You probably have a pile of it in the Colorado post office—"

"California!" Peter cried. He strode out of the post office and into the fog.

He suddenly longed for the noisy city room. Everyone there had at least known his name.

Hadn't they?

He tried to remember what they had called him. He breathed deeply. It was stupid to get so upset, he told himself. The mail would come tomorrow.

The mail didn't come, then or the next day. One morning Peter woke up feeling ill. He coughed and shivered and walked around the house with a comforter pulled about his shoulders. He wished he had gotten a phone. Then he could at least call his editors and see why none of his stories had come back.

"That's it," he whispered as he shook off the comforter. "I'll get a phone." He needed to speak with someone from the outside. He pulled on a sweater and laughed. The sound was strange to his ears. "From the outside," he murmured. "I'm talking about this town as if it were a prison."

He stepped out into bright sunshine. He looked up and down his street, almost expecting to see California adobe or Spanish colonial houses, but the brick Greystone Bay homes remained, looking less somber in the sun. Some of the curtains were open. Peter walked briskly down the sidewalk. The flags were up on the mailboxes. The mailman was running late today.

At the phone store, they told Peter it would be two weeks before they could install a phone. He gave them a deposit, arranged for a date and time, and walked outside again.

The fog had rolled in. Shivering, Peter hurried to the wharf restaurant.

"What would you like?" the waitress asked him as he sat down.

"Coffee with honey, please," he said.

"Honey? Gosh, I'll see if we have any," she said, turning away.

"Yes! Honey!" he called after her. "You had it yesterday!"

Several people turned to look at him. He picked up the paper and tried to read, but the words blurred. He wondered if he had a cold or the flu. He put his hand on his forehead; his skin was damp.

The waitress brought coffee and the little plastic bear of honey and then left without a word. Peter stared after her. He had to talk to someone who knew him.

"Mary," he whispered. He hurried to the pay phone by the rest rooms. A white "out of order" sign hung from the receiver. Peter slapped two quarters on the counter and left the restaurant.

Outside, the fog moved all around him, thick and white. He walked slowly. Buildings seemed to come and go as the fog swirled about the town. Peter tried a phone near the post office. It was out of order, too. He went from street corner to street corner, and each phone was out of order, as if everywhere the fog had been, the lines had gone down.

On the west side of town, Peter found a telephone that worked. He fumbled in his pocket for change and came up with only forty-five cents. He would have to call collect.

He stepped inside the booth and pushed 0 and then the number. "Collect from Peter," he told the operator. The phone began ringing at the other end. Peter glanced around anxiously. He could see nothing beyond the fog. He stared at the silver push-button squares. "Come on," he said, "answer the phone."

"Hello," a man said.

"Collect from Peter," the operator said. "Will you accept?"

"Peter? Just a minute," he said. "Mary! There's a collect call from a Peter."

Peter heard Mary's voice in the background. "Peter who?" she asked.

Peter slammed down the receiver. What a nasty trick, pretending she didn't know him! He kicked the phone booth. She certainly hadn't wasted any time finding someone else.

"Calm down, Peter," he told himself. "This is stupid. Call Mark. Your own brother will remember you."

He took the number from his wallet and pushed the buttons slowly. The phone began ringing.

He heard his brother's voice. "Hello?"

"Will you accept a collect call from Peter Gibson?"

"Peter!" his brother said. "Well, sure, I'll accept. How are you doing, old boy? I haven't talked to you in two years!"

"Mark," Peter sighed, leaning into the phone. "You can't imagine how good it is to hear your voice. I'm stuck out in the middle of this nasty little town working up a deep depression."

"Where are you? You didn't let us know you'd moved," Mark said.

"I wrote you last week," Peter said. "Didn't you get it? I'm in Greystone Bay."

"Greystone, eh?" Mark said. "No wonder you're depressed. I've been through there; it isn't the friendliest of places. It's not far from here, you know. Maybe two hundred miles. You should come up for Thanksgiving."

"That would be great," Peter said. "I hadn't realized we were that near to each other."

"Well, you have been somewhat of a stranger for a number of years, now, haven't you? We can fix that, though. I've got to run.

Kathy's waiting. We've got tickets to the theater. But do keep in touch. The kids would like to see their other uncle."

"I will," Peter said, smiling, hugging the phone to his shoulder.

"I'm glad you called," Mark said. "See you soon, Dave."

Mark hung up. Peter stared at the receiver. "Peter," he whispered. "I'm Peter."

He opened the door and went outside. The sun had set and it was nearly dark. Or light. He couldn't tell through the fog. He looked around until he had his bearings, and then he started home.

It was Greystone, he decided. It drained him. Or had this all started long before, when he began spending most of his time alone? He shook his head. He was being ridiculous. There were people out there who knew him, and he would hear from one of them soon. He looked down at his arms. He could hardly see them for the fog. He peered more closely at them. It was almost as if he could see right through them. His heart raced. He looked down at his chest. Was he seeing the ground through his chest? He closed his eyes. No. He was imagining all of it. He was fine, he was whole. He had just been out of touch for too long. Besides, he had a cold and his thought processes weren't functioning properly. He hurried up his road. His legs. He could barely see his legs. He wanted to scream or run. Something was not right. How could he run without legs? The fog twisted around him. The mailbox. That's it. This had all started because of the mail, but there would be mail in the box today. There had to be. Then he would be all right.

He ran. He stumbled once and his fingers touched the cobblestone. The stone was hard and slippery. He could feel it, but he couldn't see his own fingers or arms. He ran and ran. Suddenly, the shadows of the mailboxes loomed up at him, looking like the tines of a giant fork.

His hand trembled on the lip of his box as he pulled it open.
It was empty.

He opened his mouth to scream, and no sound came out.

The mail truck pulled up to the row of boxes. A child ran in front of the truck, chasing a bright red ball. Someone washing a car called to the child and waved at the mailman. He waved back. He opened the boxes one at a time and put mail inside.

When he opened Peter Gibson's box, a wisp of fog floated up into the clear blue sky and then disappeared.

"Damn fog," the mailman murmured.

He slipped a piece of mail marked "occupant" into the box and then he drove away.

At a Window Facing West

"I still can't find this place on the map," Rich said, smoothing out the coffee-stained map across the metal tabletop.

"Don't worry about it," Maggie said. She squinted as she looked out across the Gulf of California. A pelican followed the line of waves for a moment before diving into the turquoise water.

"I don't like it here," Rich said. He leaned toward Maggie and Peter and whispered, "They all seem so poor."

Maggie took a sip of beer to keep herself from saying something cruel to Rich. They should have never suggested he come along on this trip. Because Rich could not bear to stray off the beaten path, they had spent over two weeks in tacky tourist towns. He did not trust waiters who could not speak English, and he turned pale at the sight of dirty children.

Peter glanced at Maggie. She put down her glass and squeezed lemon along the rim. She wished they had been able to find limes. Of course, she supposed, they had been lucky to find a restaurant at all. And hotel rooms. She doubted that many tourists came to this place—wherever it was.

"I wish I could do something for all those poor dirty little children," Rich said. He glanced about uncomfortably.

Maggie sighed. Peter shook his head at her.

"Give them money if you think they're so poor," Maggie said. "Or throw a bucket of water over them. That should clean up a few of them."

"Don't be nasty," Peter said.

Rich pushed away from the table. "It must be nice to be so fearless, Maggie." He strode from the table and the restaurant. He stopped at the edge of the dirt road leading back to the village center and looked in either direction. A truck rumbled by and covered him with a cloud of dust.

"I hope he finds his way back to the hotel," Peter said. "He can't help the way he is, Maggie. The divorce has really shaken him."

Two boys ran up to the table. One carried a bucket of dirty water; the other held a squeegee. "Windows! Windows!" they cried together. Good thing Rich was gone, Maggie thought; these kids would scare him to death. Maggie nodded to the boys, and they ran to Peter's blue van and began washing the windows.

"Your brother has always been like this," Maggie said. "My god, he is afraid of everything."

"He's led a sheltered life," Peter said. "Ann Arbor is a long way from Mexico."

Maggie shrugged and leaned back and closed her eyes. The sun felt nice on her face. The sound of water rolling across the sand, was soothing. Now this was a vacation. She was going to stay here for a few days no matter what Rich thought.

The boys finished the windows and ran back to the table. Maggie glanced at the van as she pulled coins from the pocket of her jeans. Now the sides of the dusty van were streaked where water had run down from the windows. She gave the money to the boys, and they ran away.

"Rich is trying to be adventurous," Peter said. "He read *People's Guide to Mexico.*" Peter grinned, and Maggie laughed.

"All right, all right," Maggie said. "I'll be nice to him."

For dinner, they sat outside the same restaurant at the same table. Inside, the restaurant was crowded and noisy. Music from the jukebox came from the open windows.

"See, Rich, Bruce Springsteen. We're not that far from civilization," Maggie said. Insects buzzed around the lantern on the table. Peter stared at the flame and smiled happily as he consumed several beers. The beach became dark, except for the restaurant lights and several bonfires in the distance. Figures danced in front of the fires, black shadows against gold light.

Rich lifted his bottle of beer in salute. "You were right and I was wrong, Maggie. I am a jerk. I can't help it. A character flaw." He laughed drunkenly. "While you were out protesting the war in college, I was doing my homework. While you were marching against chemical dumps, I was doing taxes for the dumpers. I am a spineless worthless piece of crap." He laughed again.

"I wouldn't go that far," Maggie said. She sipped her beer slowly. It appeared she would be driving them back to the hotel.

"You always fight the good fight," Rich said. "You are always politically correct; I am politically incorrect. You say terrorists, I say freedom fighters. You say freedom fighters, I say guerrillas."

"Don't get her started," Peter said, lifting his head to look away from the lantern. "I don't want to hear any political speeches tonight. I want peace and quiet, beer and pretzels."

"Oh, shut up, both of you," Maggie said. "I'm sitting here trying to enjoy my beer and I'm being attacked on both sides. I stand up for what I believe in, so what?"

Peter waved a hand. "It's too late, Rich. You've started her.

She'll talk about which charities she donates to and why, and which ones you shouldn't donate to and why. She can tell you about repressed people everywhere. She's got it all right here." He tapped his head and grinned.

"The helper of the downtrodden! Patron of Mother Earth," Rich said, "we bow down to you." Rich and Peter dropped from their chairs onto the concrete porch and bowed in front of Maggie.

She laughed. "Go away. I'm trying to have a vacation."

Giggling, they pulled themselves into their chairs again. They sat quietly for several minutes. Rich drained his beer and then finished Peter's.

"We still don't know where we are," Rich said. The light from the lantern made his eyes red.

"I know where we are," Peter said.

"Mexico is not all that stable, you know," Rich continued, as if not hearing Peter. "People disappear here, too. Americans. United Statesians. Whatever we are. We disappear, too. They want our credit cards."

Maggie laughed. Rich stared angrily at her. "It's all so funny to you."

"They can have my plastic," Maggie said. "It's not really vogue for a political correspondent to carry around such things anyway."

"I think I'm going to be sick," Rich said, covering his mouth.

"Time to go home," Peter said. He stood up and put an arm across Rich's shoulder.

"You take him," Maggie said. "I'm not finished with my beer."

"Come on, Maggie," Peter said. "I've had too much to drink. You can come back after you've dropped us off if you want."

Maggie hesitated, and then she went inside the smoky restaurant to pay the bill. The conversation died for a moment as everyone stared at her. The cash register rang, and the conversations began again. Outside, Rich vomited on the left rear tire of the van.

Maggie sat at the window of their second story hotel room while Peter helped Rich into bed in his room. Their hotel was at the center of the village. Directly across the street, blocking the view of the ocean, was some sort of government building. Between the government building and the hotel was a statue of a man on a rearing horse at the center of a traffic circle. Some Mexican general. Maggie had read the inscription and then promptly forgotten it. Purple and yellow flowers grew at the back feet of the horse. No cars traveled around the circle now. A single light from the government building illuminated the man and the horse. The two boys who had washed the windows of the van sat on a nearby bench counting their money. Maggie wished she could still hear the ocean.

"He's almost asleep," Peter said as he came through the door. "He didn't want to stay alone. He's crying."

"What a baby."

Peter grabbed the doorknob and stared at her. "Sometimes you have absolutely no compassion."

Maggie turned from the window and sat on the bed.

"I wasn't expecting to babysit during our vacation," she said. "I wanted to relax and have fun."

"It hasn't been so terrible," he said. "He just gets afraid. He's never been alone. He was married to Jean right out of high school. He feels as though his entire life is crumbling."

"He shouldn't drink so much," Maggie said. "Though at least when he's drunk he's slightly amusing."

"Don't make fun of him," Peter said.

"I've made you angry," she said. "I'm sorry."

"And don't patronize me! He's known true fear; have you? I don't see you running down to Nicaragua and El Salvador, or Guatemala or any of those places you write about so eloquently. Perhaps you're just as frightened as all of us and you won't admit it. You don't really care about anything, do you? You just stay on the sidelines and write about it and pretend you're fighting the good fight." Peter pulled open the door again. "I'm staying with Rich until he feels better."

"That could be for the rest of his life," Maggie said. She sighed. "I want to explore the beach first thing tomorrow morning."

"Rich wants to leave this place," Peter said.

Maggie chewed her cheek. "Why am I being made out to be the bad guy here? I want a few days of relaxation before I go back to work. I think I've really been very accommodating to your brother."

"Good night, Maggie." Peter left, shutting the door behind him.

Maggie took off her clothes, put on a nightgown, and turned off the light. She slid under the covers. They were staying; she didn't care how Rich felt.

Maggie opened her eyes. For a moment she did not know where she was. The dark room had an unfamiliar smell—kerosene? Peter was not asleep next to her. Someone screamed.

Maggie threw off her covers and ran to the window. Below, at the center of the traffic circle, a woman struggled to get away from two men dressed in uniforms with batons and pistols strapped to their legs. Each held an arm of the woman. They spoke loudly but too rapidly for Maggie to understand. Black hair covered the woman's face as she screamed. She pulled at her hair, and her cries became desperate whimpers.

"Help me," she cried.

Maggie stepped back from the window. Had she heard those words in English or Spanish? She leaned forward slightly. The woman kicked one of the men. He pulled out his baton. He was going to hit her. Maggie covered her mouth; she felt ill. The man dropped the baton. The woman screamed again.

Maggie's heart raced. They would kill the woman if someone did not stop them. The woman had screamed for help and no one had answered. Everyone hid behind closed doors. Everyone.

Maggie had to do something, but she felt frozen in place. The woman went limp, becoming a dead weight in the men's arms. They dragged her past the rearing horse. The woman screamed again, long and loud, a pathetic wail. "Help me," she sobbed. They pulled her toward the government building and out of view of the hotel window. The sound of her cries died, and the night was quiet again. A dog barked in the distance. A seagull mewed.

Maggie stared out the window. She had watched two armed men drag someone away, and she had done nothing to stop them. The helper of the downtrodden. Patron of Mother Earth.

She had watched passively.

She backed away until the edge of the bed touched her thighs. She sat on the bed. Her legs and hands trembled.

What if they came after her next? Or Peter? She listened closely. No unusual sounds. Perhaps Rich had been right all along. Perhaps they were not safe here.

Noiselessly, Maggie packed their clothes. Then she sat on the bed and waited for sunrise.

Peter kissed her cheek, and she opened her eyes. Bright sunshine came through the open window. A warm breeze brought in the smells of the ocean.

"Sorry about last night," Peter said.

Maggie sat up. She was still nauseated.

"Did you hear anything last night?" Maggie asked.

Peter shook his head. "Not a thing. Rich's ready to explore the beach with us this morning. He's even hungry after all that drinking." Peter smiled. "Come to think of it, Rich said he thought he heard something in the night. A scream, maybe. You could ask him. Why?"

Maggie walked slowly to the window until she could just see the place where the woman and men had struggled. The scene flashed before her. She closed her eyes. What if someone had seen her watching, doing nothing? They could report her, arrest her. She breathed deeply. This was all stupid. She was in a foreign country; what could she have done?

"I thought I saw something last night, that's all," Maggie said.

"You've packed." Peter put his hands on Maggie's shoulders. "What's wrong? You look scared to death."

"I had a bad night," she snapped. She shook off his hands. "What did you expect with you in the other room while I was alone in this macho country?"

"You've never been afraid to be alone before."

"I wasn't afraid! Can we drop this?" Was the woman across the street now in that building being tortured? Maggie should go to the police and report what she saw. She should do something before it was too late.

She shivered. "I want to leave," Maggie said. "I want to go home."

Maggie lay across the back seat while Peter drove. Rich sat next to him looking out the window.

"I hope you're not leaving because of me," Rich said quietly.

"It's time to go home, that's all," Peter answered.

Maggie closed her eyes. She did not want to hear them. Peter the peacemaker. Rich the whiner. She wanted to curl up into a little ball and cry. She could have helped that woman last night, but she hadn't. She knew the woman had been destroyed. Killed, tortured, driven insane, something. All because Maggie had stood there and watched and done absolutely nothing.

She awakened in a sweat, the woman's screams echoing inside her head. She sat up. There was still something she could do to help. She could go back and tell someone what she had seen.

The idea terrified her. "Are we almost to the border?" Maggie asked.

"Soon, Maggie, soon," Peter answered.

Maggie was relieved to be in their familiar apartment again. The pictures on the walls, the carpeting, the television set, the view of the city. She ran her fingers across the kitchen table. She did not even mind that Rich had to stay a few days because his plane was not scheduled to leave until the end of the week.

"I'll make dinner," Rich said, sounding more certain of himself again. "What would you like, Maggie?"

"Sleep," she said. She smiled wearily. "I'm tired. You two stay up and have fun."

Peter turned on the television. Time for the news. Maggie quickly went into the bedroom and closed the door. She rubbed her stomach and went to the bathroom and splashed her face with cold water.

"It's not important," Maggie said as she looked at her reflection. "Whatever happened, happened; end of story." She had never seen fear in her own eyes before. It looked unnatural.

She stripped off her clothes and crawled, naked, under the covers. It would all be better after she slept.

She was in her own bed, but the window looked down upon the statue of the horse and its general. Beneath the statue, the woman lay. The horse shook itself alive and pummeled the prone woman with its hooves. Maggie backed away from the window.

"Maggie, Maggie." Peter's voice was close to her ear. "You were crying out in your sleep. Are you all right?"

Maggie opened her eyes. The room came into focus. She put her arms around Peter and held him tightly.

"Are you ever afraid?" she asked.

He laughed.

"I'm serious," she said, pulling away from him.

"Of course I'm afraid," he said. "Everyone's afraid. It's normal. That's what life is all about. What's wrong with you? You've been acting strange ever since we left Mexico. You hardly said anything in the car."

"I've never been afraid before," Maggie said. "Rich was right. I was fearless."

"Ignorant," Peter said. "You just never really looked at the world." He smoothed a strand of hair off her face. "Dinner's ready." He got up from the bed and left the room.

After a few minutes, Maggie got dressed and followed him out.

She was certain Rich knew what she had done by the way he watched her. He had heard the screams, too, even though he denied it when she asked him. He had done nothing, too. That was part of his character. It was not supposed to be part of hers. She was the fighter. The believer.

Easy to march in protests with all of those people around you, someone had told her once. Easy to believe in peace when no one holds a gun to your head. Who said that? Maggie stared at Rich across the dinner table. He had said it, hadn't he? During one of his drunken lectures in Mexico. Easy to believe when you are not afraid.

Maggie listened to the sounds of Rich and Peter eating, to the refrigerator sighing, to the traffic in the distance. Was the woman still screaming?

She did not want to sleep. She knew she would hear the screams again. She sat in her study at the typewriter. Maybe she could write about what happened to the woman. Make it part of her column. That would vindicate her. The world would know what had happened.

Maggie shook her head and turned off the typewriter. No, she knew nothing about the woman. All she could write about was her own fear and fall from grace.

She went into the darkened living room and curled up on the couch. She switched on the light and sat with her back to the curtained window. She did not want to hear or see anything as she flipped through the pages of *Vegetarian Times.*

Rich and Peter went to Disneyland the following day. Maggie kept the curtains closed and watched soap operas. She scanned the Los Angeles *Times* for any information about a missing woman in Mexico. She found nothing.

She dozed once in the afternoon and woke herself up quickly before the woman could find her. That night, she drank coffee ands read magazines at the kitchen table while Peter and Rich slept.

"Maggie, it's four in the morning," Peter said. "Why are you still up? You haven't slept in days." He rubbed his eyes and pulled out a chair and sat next to her.

"I can't," Maggie said.

"Why?"

Maggie bit her lip. Tears streamed down her face.

"I'm afraid," she said.

"Of what?" Peter asked.

"I can't tell you," she said. "You'd hate me. You'd think I was a coward."

He shook his head. "No, I wouldn't. I don't know what's wrong with you, but you've got to stop this. You don't look or sound good. So you're afraid. Don't you know that everyone is afraid? That's what life is, Maggie. Living is going on despite the fear. Rich does that every day. He's terrified, but most of the time he just faces his fears and carries on."

"But I think I may have . . ." She stopped. She could not tell him. She could not explain what she had done because she did not understand it. She had let them take away the woman and she had done nothing to stop them. "Shh," she said to Peter. "Do you hear that?"

Peter listened silently. "No, I don't hear anything," he finally said.

Maggie started to cry again. "I still hear her screaming."

Maggie waited until Peter and Rich left the apartment for the airport. Then she packed a bag and got into the car and began the drive to Mexico. Peter was right. People had to face their fears. She had to find out what had happened to the woman. Then maybe the screaming would stop.

She drove into the night. She stopped once for coffee. She heard the sounds of the woman's screams, and she quickly returned to the car and started driving again. She cried as she traveled through Mexico; Rich said it was not safe at night. She took a wrong turn and had to double back. Then she was at the village. She stopped the car in front of the police station.

She climbed out of the car. The night was quiet. The air was damp and fishy smelling. She heard the waves stroking the sand. No one screamed.

She walked into the police station. It was a small room. Two officers sat behind desks, their feet up, talking and laughing together. They both stood when she came into the room. Her legs trembled. Her vision blurred. I have to sleep, she thought; I have to eat.

"How may we help you?" one of the men asked, speaking English. She stared at them. They were the men who had taken away the woman. She put out a hand to steady herself. It was the middle of the night and she was alone with the two men who had killed the woman.

Someone screamed. Maggie looked out toward the traffic circle. It was empty.

"May we help you?" the man repeated. A baton and gun were strapped to his leg.

"I—I saw a woman here, three or four days ago," Maggie said. She slowly backed out of the office. "In the middle of the night. You took her away."

The men looked at each other, puzzled. "I am sorry but you must be mistaken," the man said. "We have no woman. Was she a friend of yours?"

The woman screamed again. Maggie put her hands over her ears. This had to stop. She stumbled out of the office.

"You look tired. Are you well?" The officer followed her into the street.

Maggie looked over at the statue. Were the horse's hooves moving? Was there blood staining the metal? I should have helped her, Maggie thought. I could have saved her. Evil flourishes where good people do nothing. Who said that? Maggie ran toward the statue. Edmund Burke? William Shakespeare? The woman screaming in her ear?

The screams were shrill, heartbreaking. Maggie shook her head as she raced toward the statue. She had to get the cries out of her brain. She had to find the woman and save her.

She stood near the horse. The world spun. The horse moved. She opened her mouth and screamed. The police officers were beside her, trying to calm her. "It's all right," they both said in Spanish. "You will be fine." Each of them took an arm. "We will take you to the hospital. You will be fine."

Maggie screamed. Fear overwhelmed her. How could she have lived her entire life without seeing—without realizing how terrifying everything was? "Help me!" she cried. She kicked the police officer. He pulled out his baton and then dropped it. The horse's bloody hooves beat the air. The woman still screamed. Maggie pulled at her hair.

"Help me!" she screamed one more time before the officers dragged her away, out of sight of the hotel window where a woman sat watching.

Fractures

Most mornings I awakened next to Lina. She would gently press herself against me or turn, half asleep, to caress my chest, and then I would know it was Lina. Usually, she pulled off her satin nightshirt and flung it across the room, laughing when it landed on the edge of the mirror where she had aimed it. Then we would make love, barely noticing the sun sifting through peach-colored blinds and bleeding pastels onto the carpet and bedspread. Sometimes she blinked and Nick was there in those pale blue eyes; other times she stiffened slightly and Teresa was in my arms. Most mornings it was just the two of us.

One morning a few days before Teresa's birthday, I opened my eyes and found Teresa sitting on the edge of the bed, staring at me, her features sullen.

"You love Lina," she said. "You wish I were gone."

"Of course I love Lina," I said, getting out of bed and stretching. The ocean was a slender strip of blue through the blinds. "I love you all, Tess. You are all the same person."

Teresa shook her head and looked down at her hands. I imagined Lina holding out her arms for me, smiling, shaking her light brown hair so that it brushed her bare shoulders.

"Remember, Adam, I met you first," Teresa said.

I went around the bed and sat next to her. She leaned against me stiffly, burying her head against me, fitting into every curve of my body. I put my arms around Teresa.

"You wish you were holding Lina, don't you?" she murmured.

I pulled away. "I'm taking a shower," I said.

I closed the bathroom door behind me and turned on the water. I knew I shouldn't get angry with her. Every year near her birthday and the anniversary of her father's death—and the "birth" of Lina and Nick—Teresa grew moody and depressed. This year her depression seemed worse, and it was affecting all of them. She told me once it was like a wound opened inside of her this time every year, reminding her that her father had died and she had broken into pieces of three. And every year, she believed that day, her twelfth birthday, would become clear to her. It never did. She did not remember a minute of that day after learning her father had died in a car accident.

I got under the shower and let the hot water massage my back. The curtain opened and Lina stood there smiling.

"Care for some company?" she asked.

She stepped into the tub and pulled me toward her.

After breakfast, Lina and I went down to the beach. The day was bright; sunshine glittered the water in white and shadowed blue. We spread a towel on the sand. Lina pulled out a sketch pad and began drawing while I lay down and put my hands beneath my head and stared up at the cloudless sky, wondering when I would finish the wood sculpture I had started a month ago. I let myself be talked into too many days on the beach. I turned on my side and watched Lina; of course Lina had been able to talk me into anything ever since I met her three years earlier.

I did meet Teresa first, at college, a few months past her

twenty-first birthday. She had just inherited the fortune her father had left in trust before he died, and a few weeks earlier, she had ended nine years of unsuccessful treatments and visits to doctors who couldn't help her. She left her mother's house and bought her own in southern California. I was majoring in art and business—I couldn't make up my mind which would be the easiest and the most profitable—at one of the few schools in California that hadn't dropped me because of poor grades. Teresa, who was in my art class, was pretty and shy and I asked her out. We had a nice dinner, but near the end of the meal I was thinking of other things and had to struggle to keep my attention on her and our dinner.

Then Lina came out. What was there about Lina? All things stirred alive when she was around, and she noticed them all even while concentrating solely on me. That night we talked for hours. At the time, I was getting pressure from family and friends for spending too much time in school or not enough time in school and generally not doing anything with my life. Lina never asked me what I "did." I fell in love almost on the spot.

Later that night I met Nick. It was certainly the strangest date I'd ever had. When Teresa took charge again, she was impressed that I liked them all and that I didn't think she was insane.

Some months later she had work started on a studio for me next to her house, and I moved in with her. It was the first time in my life that I felt settled, as if I finally had something that held my interest.

"I didn't sleep well last night," Lina said, pleasantly interrupting my reminiscences. "I dreamed of Russell. We were dancing under a hot red sky."

Russell. It had been some time since she had talked about Russell, her long-lost love. Nick had a former lover, too. The doctors claimed the lovers were not real, only metaphors for the loss of Teresa's father.

Lina put down her pencil. "It was just the two of us, Russell and me. I knew I should be happy, but I was frightened. I'm not sure why. The sky was so hot. Perhaps I was afraid he was going to melt under that sky and be lost to me. To save him, I forced myself awake, but he was gone anyway."

I turned onto my stomach. Metaphor or not, conversations about Russell bothered me. He was undefinable and untouchable, an unreal first love she would never forget. She looked off across the ocean, thinking, I knew, of him.

It was a look in her eyes I never saw when she gazed at me. It made me feel strange, that look, like an intruder in her life.

"I wish I could go to the ocean," she said.

"Lina, you are at the ocean."

"What? Oh yes. Silly me." She stood and reached for my hand. "Come on. Let's play." She pulled me up and then let go of my hand and raced away down the beach.

"I'm sorry about this morning," Teresa said, eating her fruit salad slowly. We sat in the breakfast nook looking out across the sand and ocean. Ferns moved slightly in the breeze coming through the screens.

The tiny squares of the screen muted the bright sunshine, and the day appeared hazy.

"That's all right," I said.

"It's just difficult," she said, looking down at her plate. "I thought I had accepted them as part of my life, but when I first come back and you realize Lina is gone, you seem so disappointed."

"Nonsense," I said, twirling the ice in my glass before drinking the tea. "It just takes a moment to get used to whoever is in charge."

"I want me in charge," she said. "All of the time."

"Do you want to go back to therapy?"

She shook her head. "That wouldn't do any good. I'm not crazy. I've just got two other people sharing my body."

"Right," I said. This was another way Tess had of not facing the truth. Whenever I asked her where Nick and Lina came from, she never had an answer unless I pressed her, and then she would finally sigh and say, "From my head, I guess." I wished she would go back for help. I knew if she got well, with all the personalities blended together, Lina would dominate. She'd have to: Nick was male, after all, and Teresa was so . . . unrelaxed. Lina was carefree and happy. Once she was well, her life would be easier, and Lina would realize Russell was a figment of her imagination.

Teresa looked up at me, tears in her eyes. "I want to make you happy."

I reached across the table and squeezed her hand. "You do."

"I want you to be happy with *me,* " she said.

I pushed away from the table and walked around it to her. I kissed the top of her head.

"I am happy with you," I said, resting my hands on her shoulders. "Now finish up and we'll take a walk."

I opened the door and went into the blinding sunshine and sat on the steps. Some time later, the door opened and Nick stepped out.

"Hello, Adam. How's everything going?"

I smiled. Having Nick in charge was always the most disconcerting. He was a gentle, kind person who walked and moved like someone who was accustomed to a larger body, as if he was afraid of nothing. In the twelve years Nick had been "alive" he had never gotten used to Teresa's body.

"Hello, Nick," I said. "Out a little early today?"

He nodded. "I guess so. Anything wrong with Teresa?"

We started walking down the beach together. "She was a little depressed this morning," I answered. "She was complaining about not being in control enough."

Nick shook his head. I knew none of them had control over their comings and goings, and none were aware of the other ones, except through secondhand information. They each came into and out of existence, usually dividing the waking hours into three sections.

"I was surprised not to see you last night," I told him. "Lina and I had a good time, though. We danced all night."

"You may have been surprised, but I bet you weren't disappointed," he said, grinning. I laughed.

He stopped, bent over, and picked up a stone. He turned it slowly in his hand once and then threw it at the ocean. "Laura could dance," he said. "I was so clumsy, but she taught me how. I liked it best when she stopped and danced by herself to show me a step. She was so graceful." He smiled. "I would like to dance with her again someday. You know, our families didn't approve of us, so we had to sneak around."

"Oh?" This was new. When Nick and Lina came into being, they hadn't even had names until Teresa's mother gave them ones. As time passed, they had invented their past loves, Russell and Laura, but they had never before gone into specifics about them.

"Why didn't your folks approve?" I asked.

He shrugged. "I don't know. Maybe we just thought they didn't approve, to make it more exciting. And it was so exciting when we were together, and painful. Every moment was so excruciating; the longing was so intense." He glanced at me and then back at the ocean. "But that was a long time ago, wasn't it?"

He turned to me again, and Teresa was there, crying.

"I want to go to the ocean," she said, holding out her hand to me. "I want to go home."

That night I awakened to the sound of crying next to me. I put my arm under her shoulder and drew her close, not certain who it was I held. I stroked her hair and told her everything would be all right. She turned to me and pulled at my clothes and kissed me hard. I slipped her nightgown over her head, kissing her, caressing her. As I entered her, I whispered, "Lina," and her body tightened and she began crying again. "It's Tess, Adam, Tess." Then she relaxed and pushed against me, moving, undulating, whispering in my ear. Only it wasn't Teresa, or Lina, it was Nick, calling out to Laura. I moved over him, trying not to hear; then I looked down and it was Lina, holding me, smiling, whispering. I put my head near her lips, wanting to hear her words as we moved together, and then I wanted to cry, feeling Lina's skin against mine as she whispered another man's name.

Before falling asleep again, they told me they wanted to go home. I lay awake listening to them breathing quietly next to me. I had tried to take this relationship as it came, to accept it as normal. But it wasn't normal. I had just made love to three different people in the same body. I shook my head. No, that was wrong. They were all one person and I loved that person. I closed my eyes and tried to sleep. I wanted her well. Perhaps a trip back home would help her. She hadn't been back to Canyons since she and her mother left after her father's funeral. Perhaps she wanted to go back after all this time because a breakthrough was imminent.

I slid out of bed and quietly packed for our trip. I woke them up before dawn. At the lavish breakfast I had prepared, all three took turns coming out. Each seemed excited about the trip.

On the road, Lina was her usual self again, laughing and cuddling, pointing out things on 101 that caught her attention. The highway twisted around the coast. Midday, Teresa sat next to me watching the water. The coast became more rugged and jagged, with enormous rocks jutting out of the water. In the afternoon, the air grew cooler and damp and the highway wove into dark green-black forests where moss hung from the branches like spider webs in an empty house. When the trees parted, foamy waves crashed against the rock and beaches.

In the late afternoon, Nick was sitting next to me.

"It smells like home," he said, watching the trees go by.

Two hours later we pulled into Canyons. "It's so different," Nick said. "The only thing I recognize is the smell."

I found a motel on the road near the beach and checked us in. After we unpacked our clothes, Teresa was in charge.

She slipped on her jacket and waved to me, uncharacteristically impatient.

"Come on," she said. "I want to show you my old house."

Most of the homes had the dilapidated look of beach houses, bent from the constant wind, exteriors streaked with rust and moss. Teresa's house was on a bluff overlooking the ocean. I slowed the car so she could look at it.

"That was my room up to the right," she said. "It's a lot bigger than I remember. Isn't it supposed to look smaller because I'm older?" She laughed and I smiled. "It does look older and it's a different color. I wonder who lives in there now?"

"Do you want to go inside?"

"No," she said. "Let's go to the ruins instead."

"The ruins?"

"Just turn the car around and drive about a mile," she said.

I drove until Teresa told me to stop. Then I pulled the car off to the side of the road and we walked to a bluff that had been windswept clear of grass; the ruddy earth had a sheen to it.

"Where are the ruins?" I asked, seeing nothing but dirt.

"This is all part of the ruins," she said, pulling her coat close around her and turning from the icy northern wind. "There used to be lots of buildings here. It was like the Barbary Coast, only not as famous. People came out of the wilderness and from towns all over on the weekends. There were dances and parties."

I followed as she walked around. The land dipped. We stood

looking down at a rectangular foundation. Muddy water and sand lay in one end of it.

"This was a pool," she said. "Over there, if we were a little closer, you could see a brick structure on the hill; that's where they pumped up sea water and then heated it for the pool."

"What happened to everything?"

"It all burned to the ground in 1936 and they never rebuilt. Here, look." She kicked at the ground. Shards of glass were everywhere, embedded in the ground. "This is where the dance hall was, right next to the pool. There are charred beams around here, too, somewhere, just the ends of them sticking out of the ground." She looked about her. "It doesn't look like much now, but at night it's magical. Some people believe it's haunted. The moon and stars and fog reshape everything, and it's easy to imagine what it was like. My friends and I used to come here at night and hold seances." She smiled. I wondered what Lina would think of the ruins.

"I came here the night my dad died. I'd forgotten that," she murmured. "We should come back here when it's dark, Adam. You'd really see what it was like."

"Sure, we'll come out," I said. "Perhaps it'll be warmer at night."

"You're cold?" she asked, rubbing my arms. "Let's go inland a bit then. I've had enough for now."

Nick came out as we sat in a restaurant overlooking the ocean. The sun was just setting, shadowing the beach in shades of pink and purple. The sand grayed, and I could barely make out the shapes of pelicans standing by a small stream running into the ocean. Nick stared out the window.

"Is it as you remember it?" I asked.

He shook his head. "It's all different. It can't be the right place."

"This is Canyons," I said, wishing Lina would come out and share the sunset with me.

"I thought if we came back here . . ." he began. "I thought I could find Laura again." He picked up his fork and pushed his salad around with it. "But this is not the place." He closed his eyes. "I don't want to be here."

"Nick." I touched his hand. He opened his eyes and Lina was there.

"Where are we?"

"In a restaurant in Canyons," I said.

"Canyons?" She looked out the window. The sun was gone and the beach was hazy; only the curling whites of waves could be seen.

"Do you recognize it?"

"Not from here," she answered.

"When we're finished, I'll show you around."

As we drove through the town, Lina sat against the door, reminding me of Teresa. She turned to me often and smiled nervously.

"I feel funny," she said. "I don't know this place."

I took her by Teresa's old school and house. Then I drove past the ruins.

"I guess there was a dance hall here and a heated swimming pool," I told her, stopping the car.

I looked over at her. She was shivering slightly. The day was graying into black, and her features were indistinct.

"Can we go back to our room?" she asked. "I'm tired."

I smiled. "Not used to being around this time of night, eh?"

"I guess not."

I reached over and embraced her. She held on to me tightly. "I wish you could be around always," I whispered. She squeezed me and then pulled away. There were tears in her eyes.

"What's wrong, babe?"

She turned her face to the window.

"It's just not what I expected," she said.

I remembered what Nick had said about expecting to find Laura; perhaps Lina thought she would find Russell, too. I breathed deeply, telling myself it was stupid to be jealous. Obviously, by coming home, they all thought they'd find what they had lost: Teresa's father. But he was dead. Maybe now they would all realize it. If his death was accepted, perhaps the pieces could be put together again into one person.

"I'll take you back now," I said.

Someone shook me awake. In the darkness I couldn't tell how they held her body, so I didn't know who it was.

"Let's go now," they whispered.

"Where?"

"To the ruins."

"What time is it?"

"I'm not sure. After midnight."

After midnight? The anniversary of their father's death. I got out of bed quickly and dressed.

The ride was short. I parked the car and got out, hurrying to keep up with Lina/Nick/Tess.

The wind had died. Overhead, a full moon sharpened the shadows. Below, the ocean moved, its waves like snakes sliding across the sand. A mist settled around the ruins. Teresa was right; it was different. I could almost imagine a dance hall.

"See." It was Teresa. "Anything could happen here."

Where the wind had eroded the earth, the red ground looked alien, a Martian landscape at night.

"I felt safe here," she said. "This place gave most people the creeps. But I always liked it."

Something shifted and everything was slightly different. The mist moved, more like thick smoke than fog. It shaped itself into a building.

"Tess, do you see that?"

"I know this place." Lina.

I blinked hard. Lina moved closer to the apparition. When I put my hand on her arm, she shook me away.

"I know this place," she said again.

The image of the hall wavered, and then two people were inside dancing. I squinted. Lina stopped. I moved closer until I was standing at what would have been a wall, but there wasn't one. It was only mist that seemed to swirl around the dancers, moving to form other people and then floating away again, never solidifying. The two dancers were clear, the woman dressed in an apricot-colored dress, the man in a dark suit. The woman stopped to show the man a step. I stopped breathing. I knew her smile, her walk, the toss of her head: They were all Lina's movements.

I touched Lina's arm to reassure myself she was there.

"Russell," Lina whispered, staring at the man.

The couple began dancing again. The other shapes moved around them. Lina glanced up at the sky. I followed her gaze.

The mist roof was aflame. The dance hall was burning again, just as it had in 1936. I stepped away and pulled Lina with me.

"No!" It was Nick. He pried my fingers from his arm. The dancing couple was smiling, gazing intently at one another. The man. I knew him, too. I looked back at Nick.

"Laura!" he called.

Laura? Russell? What was happening? He started to run toward them. I jumped in his path and put my arms around him to hold him still.

"Russell!" Lina screamed.

The roof cracked. Lina tore loose from me and ran for the building. I leaped and caught her in the mist wall. The sudden heat was tremendous. I heard screams, the sounds of music dying away; smoke seemed to fill my lungs. Then there was a noise—like air being sucked from a tube, or from Lina's body, and then she went limp in my arms. I pulled her away from the building. The couple looked up. The man swore and took the woman's hand. They ran toward us.

"They're gone," Teresa whispered. "Really gone."

I didn't know what she meant; I could still see them coming through the mist. I looked at her and then back at the couple and something clicked into place and I understood. Lina and Nick were no longer a part of Teresa. They were in the dance hall, becoming the people they had once been: Laura and Russell, the long-lost lovers.

The dance hall was burning down around them.

"Oh God!" I cried rushing toward the building.

Lina/Laura stumbled. Russell/Nick pulled her up. They were like two bright lights amidst the rushing white shadows. The roof creaked. Teresa grabbed me. The roof started to fall. Lina/Laura looked at me an instant before the ceiling fell.

"Lina!" I screamed.

The night sky was red, melting all that was real.

And then the mist cleared. Teresa and I were standing on the empty bluff on a starlit night. I ran around the place where the hall had been.

"It's gone, Adam," Teresa said. "They're gone."

I shook my head. Teresa held me still.

"I remember now," she said. "The same thing happened that night. I came here after I found out my father was dead. I was so upset, and when the dance hall appeared, I didn't really know what I was seeing—I still don't. The woman was showing the man how to dance, and then they looked like they were in trouble. I wanted to help, I guess. I ran toward them and they ran to me. I felt something peculiar, like air passing through me, or something. Then the dance hall disappeared. Something must have happened as we ran toward each other. We somehow got mixed up in one another. Ghosts? Now they're gone. It's over! It can be just you and me now."

I looked down at her and wanted to scream. She gazed steadily at me.

"So I was right all this time," she said, letting me go. "You do only love her."

"We can get her back," I said.

"She's dead," Teresa said. "She was just a ghost, someone who died in the fire."

"No, they weren't ghosts. Didn't you feel the fire, hear the music, see them clearly? They were *real,* Tess. I don't know how, but they were. Maybe there is some sort of connection here between the past and the present. Maybe we were looking into the past. Twelve years ago Lina and Nick came out of the past—"

"—and invaded my body? I don't care what the explanation is," Teresa said. "I'm just grateful it's over."

"We can come back another night," I said. "We could catch Lina before she dies, bring her back here."

"No! I won't go through that again. Twelve years of living only a few hours a day."

I took her by the shoulders. "But this time you would know what was happening! You'd know you weren't crazy."

"I would still be sharing my life, and I would still know you'd rather be with her." She pulled away.

"You saved her once," I said. "If there's a chance of saving her life again, won't you try? You've lived with her for twelve years. Don't you feel anything for her?"

"You've lived with them; I don't know them. I do know they are responsible for large portions of my life being gone. And if you care so much about *them* how come you only mention Lina? Don't you care what happens to Nick? I won't do it, Adam You can have me, but only me."

She turned and ran to the car. I sank onto the ground and put my head in my hands.

The next day we walked around town. Teresa was happy. As I watched her, I realized I had never really seen her happy before. I tried to be pleasant, but I was thinking of the night before, trying to figure out a way to get Lina back. We stopped at the historical museum. Teresa hurried through the exhibit of the fire. I stopped and looked at old pictures of the dance hall. It was just as I had seen it last night, before it burned. I flipped through an old newspaper describing the fire. Although the fire had swept the town, only three people had died: an old man who wouldn't leave his house and two people in the dance hall. I felt the room close in on me as I read their names: Laura and Russell Myers. They had been married the morning of the fire. Their faces looked out from the picture, Nick's grin and Lina's smile. I gently touched the faded photo, and then I left the museum.

The day passed slowly. That night, Teresa made love to me far more passionately than she ever had before. I closed my eyes, and she kissed the tears away.

Just before midnight I slipped out of bed and left the room quietly and drove to the ruins. I stood on the bluff hoping the dance hall would appear again, hoping desperately that the burning of the dance hall was a nightly ritual that I could somehow tap into again.

The mist gathered. A seagull screamed. I would get Lina back, I told myself. I would go into the dance hall and get her out before the ceiling caved in. Somehow I would save her.

The mist shaped itself into the hall. I pleaded out loud for Lina to come back. Then they were there, Lina and Nick, dancing together, holding each other closely. "Lina!" I called, running toward them. The mist eddied. I looked around. I was standing in shadow and mist, nothing else. When I moved back I could see the hall and the couple dancing. I tried getting inside again and again, but nothing happened. Then I remembered what Teresa had said: It had happened exactly the same both times. She had run toward the dance hall and into the mist at a particular time. Perhaps there were only a few minutes when the two worlds were accessible to one another. That's why Lina could be standing next to me and watching herself at the same time: In the past, she had not yet plunged into our time.

I watched them. Lina stopped to show Nick a step. I moved closer to the wall. Now I could smell smoke. Fire burned. I leaned into the wall. People screamed. The roof creaked. Nick and Lina looked up and then grasped hands and raced toward me, not seeing me. I could see them and their determined, terrified faces: They were not going to let this happen to them. I ran to them, my arms outstretched. "This way!" I cried. We passed through one another, and I felt a comforting shiver run down my back, as if Lina had gently touched my spine with the tip of her finger.

I stepped back and the roof fell. Then I screamed into the empty mist.

I opened my eyes. Morning light painted the breakfast nook in smoky shades of blue. I held a croissant in my hand. Teresa sat across from me, laughing. Her laughter died gradually into a smile as she realized I was now in charge.

"Hello, Adam," she said, tearing her roll in half and buttering it. "Nick—I mean Russell—was just telling me a funny story."

I looked down at my plate. Russell again. Two months ago she had been so in love with me. That was before she met Russell/Nick.

"How is Lina?" I asked.

"*Laura* is fine," she said. "She's finally getting accustomed to the new body, your body." She smiled slightly. "She even taught me to dance yesterday, and then Nick and I danced all night."

Lina. If only I could unlock my mind and reach her. If only Teresa could see me again when she looked at me.

"Tess—" I began, my voice trembling.

"Finish your breakfast," she said, standing up and looking slightly annoyed. "It's a lovely day. I'll meet you outside and we can take a walk. All right, darling?"

She touched my shoulders and kissed the top of my head lightly, distractedly, as if she were thinking of something—or someone—else.

She walked outside and let the screen door slam away the light as she left.

Hollows

Faith opened up the house when she first arrived on the West Coast. She wanted light, fresh air, sound. She could smell the ocean just below the bluff and hear waves pounding shale. Occasionally someone in a car, usually a tourist, drove down the twisted dirt road to look at the lighthouse that sat almost in Faith's backyard. Sometimes Faith stood outside and waved to the cars, trying to step back into life.

It didn't work. She missed her husband, Jack. She heard him in every sigh of the house he had never been in. She saw him in every shadow in the woods east of her house. And at night, she felt the emptiness against her breasts, stomach, and thighs where she used to spoon up against him.

So she closed her windows and curtains and tried to forget the world. Tried to forget her husband was dead.

When she went for her mail at the post office, Mr. Winters, the postmaster, talked to her about the latest local death, birth, marriage, or divorce. Faith listened politely as she threw away her junk mail. She never knew who the people were he spoke about, and she didn't care.

"You okay way out there by yourself?" he would often ask. "You're awfully young to be so alone."

"I'm fine," she would tell him. Smiling. Trying to be polite. She wasn't that young: old enough to have a dead husband.

Later, when she got home from the post office, she usually threw away the rest of the mail, especially those letters from her family back home in the East. She didn't want to hear about anyone else's happiness or unhappiness. The bills she paid. Once in a while, she wondered what she'd do when she ran out of money.

One night she awakened from a dream to darkness and thought she was not alone. The thought comforted her until she remembered her dream. Jack was alive, and they lay together on the couch in their home in Michigan, giggling as they took off each other's clothes. He was close to her. Their hearts beating together.

Then she opened her eyes to the darkness. She put her hands between her legs, curled into a ball, and cried until she fell to sleep again.

The next morning, the rabbit ran by her window. It looked half-dead, its coat matted with blood. Faith stepped out the kitchen door into the misty rain. The rabbit stopped when the door opened. Faith knelt down on the wet earth, and the rabbit hopped over to her. She laid her hand gently on its back and tried to smooth down the fur. The rabbit stared at her. It was so still. Not like any rabbit she had ever seen.

A car came down the dirt road. Startled, the rabbit ran away.

When Faith went to get the mail that day, Mr. Winters told her about Betsy Cramer's divorce and poor Mary Downer's boy Kevin killing himself. Faith smiled, took her mail, and went home again. Outside her back door, a gray gelding stood looking toward the ocean. Faith went to him and petted his back. He remained in the backyard all afternoon. Faith brought a book and chair outside and stayed with the horse until he wandered away toward dusk. She wondered if he was sick. She hadn't seen it graze all day.

That night, she had empty dreams, nightmares about the hollow places in her life.

She awakened to a knock on the kitchen door. She quickly pulled on jeans and a shirt and went to the door and opened it.

A young man stood in the rain. His face, hands, and bright red hair were dirty.

"Are you all right?" she asked. He looked as though he had been in a car accident. She thought of Jack lost in all that twisted metal. She opened the screen door. "Are you all right?" she asked again. "You look like you're in shock. Come in. Sit down. Can I call someone?"

He came into the house and sat in a chair at the table. He shook his head. "No, I think I'm all right." He spoke haltingly. Faith wondered if she should try and find some identification on him and call someone. She went to the door and looked out. No car. She looked back at the table. The man stared at her.

"May I stay here?" he asked.

Faith looked around the dark house and thought of her empty dreams and said, "Yes."

She made tea and gave him a cup. It seemed to revive him a bit. She took him to the bathroom and gave him a towel. He stared at her, so she showed him how the old shower worked.

"It's tricky," she said. He began unbuttoning his clothes. She quickly left the room. She pulled a box of Jack's clothes down from the closet. She took out jeans and a shirt and hung them on the outside of the bathroom door.

She made breakfast and wondered why she had let a stranger into her house. She knew why: she wasn't afraid of him or anything else. What could he do to her? Nothing could make her hurt anymore than she already did.

He came to the kitchen in Jack's clothes. She wanted to cry, but she gave him food instead.

"My name is Faith," she told him.

The man looked around the room, unsure of himself, it seemed. "Tom. My name is Tom. Is this what you wanted?"

"Pardon me?" she asked.

He stared at her. She smiled. He smiled and reached across the table to touch her hand. Startled, she put her hands in her lap.

"Can I call someone for you?" she asked.

"I just want to stay here for a while," he said. "If that's all right."

She nodded.

He sat with her all day, flipping slowly through magazines while she read. It was strange having another body in the house. When she looked over at him, he smiled at her. At lunch, she talked to him about people he didn't know. She enjoyed the talking anyway. At dinner, she read him letters Jack had written to her before they were married. She brought him a blanket and pillow when it got dark and told him he could sleep on the couch.

He reached for her hand again and said, "Is this what you want?"

She shook her head. She thought of her empty bed, of Jack pressing against her, and she wanted to scream.

She sat on the couch next to Tom. He unbuttoned her blouse as she reached to turn off the lamp. Then she stood and took off her jeans. She saw his hands move toward his shirt in the semi-darkness. "No, leave it on," she whispered. She wanted to smell Jack in his shirt, feel a part of him in the cloth.

She opened herself to him, and he gently pushed into her. Her heart raced. She unbuttoned his shirt, grasped it tightly, and pressed her breasts against his. She started to cry as he moved faster, against her, in her, she wanted him to go deeper, reach inside her, touch her heart and bring her back to life again. He kissed her neck and she shivered. "I love you," he said as he moved in her, as she climaxed, Jack's body against hers in her mind's eye.

Then he lay gently on top of her, for just a moment, and all the hollow places disappeared.

In the morning, Faith awakened with Tom next to her. He smiled and leaned over and kissed her stomach.

"Good morning," she said.

"Is this what you want?" he asked.

"I don't know what you mean by that," she said, "but I guess this is what I want." She suddenly had an urge to open the curtains, let in the light. She got off the couch and stretched. "I haven't gotten the mail in two days. The postmaster is liable to send out a posse. I better go. You want to come?"

He shook his head.

She slipped on her clothes. "Will you be here when I come back?" she asked.

"Yes."

She smiled and leaned down to kiss him. He took her hand in his. The sleeve of Jack's shirt fell away from his arm, revealing a long thick red line down his arm.

"Does that hurt?" she asked.

"No," he answered.

"A man of few words," she said. She went to the door, grabbed her purse from the counter, and waved good-bye to him. "I'll be back."

Mr. Winters told her he had missed her. Betsy Cramer was having second thoughts about her divorce and, funny thing, Old Man Cooper's horse disappeared from the barn hours after it had died and the body of Mary Downer's carrot-haired son Kevin, the one who had killed himself, disappeared from the funeral parlor. A grave robber on the loose?

Faith thought of the horse she had seen day before yesterday. Staring at her. Like the rabbit. Asking her with those big brown eyes if this was what she needed to make her happy.

"He was a good kid, Kevin was," Mr. Winters said. "Kind of lost though. Slit his arms open."

Faith remembered Tom pressed against her, inside of her, her heart pounding alone.

She drove home and found Tom sitting at the kitchen table. A patch of skin had fallen away from his face.

"I scratched it on mistake," he said.

"Who are you?" she asked. Thinking of him inside her. Dead.

"I don't know," he said. "Part of this house. The land. You weren't at rest. I had to find some form that would comfort you."

"But you're dead," she said.

He looked at her. "I thought you were, too."

She stared at him. "I suppose I was," she finally said.

She went to the table and sat next to him. Maybe she could take him—whatever he was—back home to Jack's decaying body and make him come alive again. Tom blinked and another patch of skin fell from his face. No. That would not work.

She leaned over and kissed his cheek. "Thank you. You can go now. I'm all right."

He nodded, touched her hand lightly, and walked out of the house and into the day. Faith stood and watched him disappear into the woods.

Then she opened all the curtains and windows in the house. As she packed her bags, she wondered if Mr. Winters would soon be talking about her, the nice lady who used to live on Lighthouse Road. She hoped he found someone else to talk to.

She took her bags out to the car, put them inside, and then turned to look at the house. She pressed her hands against her breasts, hugging herself. She smiled. The hollow places didn't seem as empty as they had been.

She got into the car and drove away from the house, east, toward home.

The Black Wallpaper

Abraham Van Helsing's Journal—

15 October.—Today we leave London for the country in the hopes of curing my beloved Catherine of her melancholy. We have not discovered the cause of it as yet, although her physician and I have interviewed Catherine at length.

When Dr. Hawkins finally diagnosed Catherine's lassitude as melancholia, he recommended taking her away from London's nearly constant autumn fog. He was alarmed that I allowed Catherine to read the London newspapers—this meant she was aware of the murders which had recently occurred in the East End. I assured him Catherine was a modern woman and no newspaper article would cause her to blush or faint away.

"Mrs. Van Helsing was my assistant in my medical practice in Amsterdam when we were first married," I reminded him. "I relied on her exceptional brain and steady hand for many years."

After helping me in my practice, Catherine blessed our lives by giving birth to our sweet boy Abraham. When Abraham was five, we moved to London to enable me to continue my studies with the esteemed metaphysician Dr. Ehrenreich. After a time, he asked me to stay on as his assistant. For many years we have lived happily, the three of us—Catherine, Abraham, and myself—in a cocoon of blissful domesticity interrupted only by my sojourns to the university each day.

As summer came to a close this year, however, Catherine began calling out in her sleep. I could not understand her words, try as I might. When I awakened her, she had no memory of her outbursts. Then she stopped sleeping regularly.

"A form of hysteria, perhaps," Dr. Hawkins suggested. "You should have consulted me earlier, Van Helsing. As a physician yourself you know these conditions can deteriorate quickly."

And as a physician, I did not believe the diagnosis of hysteria was the correct one. This disease was particular to the Americas and not one with which our European women were often afflicted. I did, however, concur about the melancholy.

I have rented an old English manor house, which shall be fun for us all. Catherine asked if we could please have plenty of trees, flowers, and sunlight.

"Sunlight in October, my dear," I said, "may be difficult to obtain. Most of the blossoms are in wilt or gone all together. But the trees shall stand tall—I am certain they are covered in autumn color. You shall revive immediately!"

I am looking forward to seeing Catherine's smile once again.

16 October.—Catherine sits beside me in the breakfast room which overlooks the garden. The French doors open and a slight breeze ruffles Catherine's hair as she takes the medicine I have given her. Today she has color in her cheeks. Abraham squirms in his seat. He has finished breakfast but waits for consent to leave.

Finally I look over at the boy and say, "You may be excused, Abraham. Miss Deirdre is waiting to give you your lessons."

"Oh please, Father," says my nine year old son. "Can't I go outside? There is no rain!"

Catherine looks up and smiles. "Yes, Father," she says. "There is no rain. We should all go outside and play."

I cannot resist her smile—or the boy's. I motion him to go outside.

"Thank you, sir!" He jumps up, kisses his mother's cheek, then is gone.

Catherine pats my hand.

"Feeling better this morning?" I ask. "You slept well?"

"What else could I do but sleep?" she says. "I am not allowed to read, write, paint, or supervise the staff or my child. Sleep is the only alternative."

"You are supposed to be resting. You need to get your strength back."

"Yes, Abraham. Did you notice the wallpaper in my bedroom? It's so bright. Even in the dark. As if it is constantly reflecting light from some source I cannot discern." She looks around the room. "It is strangely quiet here. And bright."

"You asked for sunlight."

"But it isn't sunlight," she says. "It is just . . . the light hurts my eyes."

She shrugs. Her shoulders look so delicate. She has lost weight and has become weak, so unlike herself when she is in good health.

"Good, that is what we need!" I say briskly. "Light. And pleasant thoughts!"

"By the by, good Abraham," Catherine says, "don't you think it is going a bit too far to tell the staff to keep newspapers away from me? I am not a child."

I blush. "I know. I am trying to do as Dr. Hawkins instructed."

"You are a doctor, too," Catherine says. "Does your intuition tell you that keeping me from the world will cure me?"

I laugh. "I am a man of science, sweet Kate! Intuition is part of a woman's domain."

"My intuition tells me I need to have some activity to keep me busy or I shall go mad! Couldn't I write in my journal?"

"That is a reasonable request," I say. "I will consult with the doctor."

She sighs.

"Dearest, you requested my assistance. Do you not remember? After you had not slept for a week, you put your hand in mine and begged me to help you. That is all I am attempting to do."

"Father!" My son comes running into the room. "Come quick. I've found a yellow and green snake!"

"I shall join you," I say.

My son runs outside again. I kiss the top of Catherine's head. "Perhaps you would like to come out with us?"

"As soon as I finish my tea," she says. "Did you find out what happened to the trees?"

"I talked to the vicar last night," I say. "He told me a strange rot came over the trees a few weeks ago, and they had to chop them all down."

"It was so strange," Catherine says wistfully, "coming down the drive and seeing stump after stump of dead trees. Now there are so few trees on the property. Do you suppose it is a sign?"

"A sign of what?"

"That nothing will ever be the same," she says. "I had everything I wanted, husband. And now. I wished for trees, and they were taken away from me. Perhaps it is a sign to remind me that I am now vulnerable, and everything around me is likewise vulnerable."

"Life is not that personal, Catherine," I say. "When we worked side by side in the clinic, you saw sickness strike down the noblest of person yet pass by those who were lost in drunken debauchery. Illness is of the brain or blood, inherited from our families or caused by our living environment. The trees became diseased. That is all."

"Still," she says, "I feel that all is not right here." She looks over at me and smiles. "Never mind that. Your son awaits you. Go."

"I will instruct the gardener to begin planting more trees immediately," I say to Catherine before I leave, but she is no longer listening, lost in her melancholy again.

Catherine Van Helsing's Journal—

19 Oct.—At long last! I can once more set my thoughts to paper. I cannot honestly converse with anyone here. I feel alone and lonely out in this small town in the English countryside— even though I have seen none of the country. I have been only in this house and the gardens. I wish I could summon back my strength—it continues to seep away since I saw what I saw. But I cannot speak or write of it yet. Maybe not ever. I wish not to think on it at all. Can I hide from the experience? Will the consequences of what I saw then be lessened?

This place is far too big for the three of us and the servants. My husband says he can do his work here. I suspect he will start traveling to London during the weekdays, and I will be left even more alone.

Perhaps I will feel freer with him gone. Not to be watched all the time. During those few moments I am alone with my boy Abraham that I feel myself again. Only then. We sit on the floor or on the earth in the garden, laugh, and tell each other stories. I would do anything for him. For his father, as well. I would protect them with my life. Only just now I feel so physically weak. It is as though I have seen the truth of the world, and my physical body cannot bear it! My mind does not waver, however, despite what the doctor tells Abraham.

I am not sleeping through the night again. I think it is the wallpaper. It is as though a light is on all night in my room. I have asked Abraham to replace the paper. I chose a darker pattern, an almost rosy maroon and gray. They shall put it up soon.

I wish Abraham would sleep in my room, but he says the doctor has told him we must abstain from marital relations. I suggested he come and sleep next to me. He thought this was a bizarre request. My poor dear husband! I love him, but he is so conventional.

The vicar and his wife came over for tea yesterday. Why is it I can never remember their names? I shall call them Mr. and Mrs. Vicar, instead. Or perhaps not—this might alarm Abraham!

I asked them about the history of the house. They could not tell me much, except that one family owned it for a very long time, and they were prosperous and loved one another dearly. It was sold a few years ago to a gentlemen and his wife; they came only in the summers, and no one saw much of them.

"I'm not certain who owns the place now," Mrs. Vicar said, "but I know the gardener has had a terrible time lately with various plant diseases. There was a blight on the rhododendrons. He had to pull them all up. Then the trees."

"Yes," Mr. Vicar said, "but it has all worked out the better for *your* family. It's much sunnier in here now than it used to be. Quite pleasant."

"Yes," Mrs. Vicar agreed. "Quite."

Abraham Van Helsing's Journal—

28 October.—Catherine is much improved. She was laughing and playing with Abraham this morning. Perhaps I could go into London for a few days, after all. Dr. Ehrenreich has a brain fever patient he wants me to examine. The man was a loving husband

one day, and then he became ill. Since his recovery, he has started drinking and beating his wife and children. No doubt, this case will confirm what I already believe. Men are not evil. They become diseased—a brain is damaged, so a man's personality is altered. He is not possessed, he has not been cursed, he is a victim of circumstance—and that circumstance is disease.

Catherine seemed particularly interested in this case.

"You are certain a fever caused this change?" she asked me.

"I have not examined the patient yet," I answered, "but from the facts given to me, yes, I am fairly certain. What other cause? A person's personality and demeanor do not alter suddenly without some organic cause."

Catherine stared out at the garden. My son Abraham sat on a bench outside reading. She waved to him when he looked up.

"You don't believe in evil?" she asked, turning to look at me.

"I believe evil happens, but it is done by men," I said.

"Not by women?" She smiled.

"Rarely," I said. "Do I believe in an evil such as Satan? You know the answer to that, my dear."

"What if I told you I have seen evil?" she whispered.

I went over to her and put my arm around her waist. "The doctor told you you mustn't brood."

"I'm not brooding, husband. I am telling you that I believe in evil as separate from people, and I have seen it. That is how I know. I don't think I did believe it until then."

"Catherine, you must stop this. The doctor told you—"

"I think I shall have Abraham read to me," Catherine said abruptly.

"But, Catherine, we were talking."

She stopped and looked at me. "No, I was talking, but you were not listening. Go to London. Do what you need to do. Abraham and I will wait for you here."

After this conversation, strangely enough, Catherine seemed cheered. She laughed and ate dinner with enthusiasm. She even played the piano for us. Chopin, I believe. The new wallpaper was installed yesterday. Catherine has not said a word about it.

Catherine Van Helsing's Journal—

30 Oct.—Abraham has left for London. My son and I are alone with the servants. We will celebrate All Hallow's Eve with them. Maryann says they will make a feast, then a fire outside. I have given them permission to build a fire on the other side of the house, in the clearing. I saw what looked like a fire ring there, so it must have been used before.

I decided not to take the medicines while Abraham is gone. They make me feel strange and dry out my mouth. Last night I stared at the new wallpaper until I fell to sleep. The paper was not as dark as I would have liked, but it was better than what was there before. I cannot remember what color it had been, only that it was too bright.

Abraham tells me not to think "dark" thoughts. He is naive. He believes that life is basically fair and good, and if we are good and decent people, all will be well. He is wrong. I happened to be in a carriage in a neighborhood I did not normally frequent when everything changed for me. When I saw "it." When I understood reality to be different from what I had perceived it to be. I knew in that moment that I was in jeopardy. That both my Abrahams were in jeopardy. Now and forever. Since that encounter I have felt so weak. I cannot shake this lassitude. And I must. Because this evil is not a singular thing. It may be everywhere.

I am afraid part of it may have latched onto me that day, followed me here, and is now in this house. I don't know! I am no longer certain of anything. I still cannot write of what I saw. Perhaps if I did write it all down, the power would go out of the experience. After all, when I think on it, it was such an ordinary occurrence. How could it then make a wreck of my life?

Whatever it was, whatever happened to me, I must rally, so that I can protect myself and my family from harm!

2 Nov.—Abraham Sr. would be quite cross if he knew what his son and I did last night. I ate far more food than anyone should, then went outside under a nearly full moon and danced around the fire. Everyone sang. I did not know the words, but it didn't matter. Abraham Jr. was so happy! He learned the songs right away. They were all very kind to him. Before we left the celebration, one of the men made a toast to our good health. I appreciated the gesture. Everyone looked sincere with raised glasses, cheeks rosy from the fire (or drink), asking that we might be well. I felt as though I might carry on after all.

I fell directly to sleep that night. When I awakened in the morning and looked around my bed chamber, all appeared normal. Even the maroon roses on the wallpaper seemed to be as they should be.

The next day, I felt well enough to explore the house. Abraham Jr. was upstairs having his lessons, so after breakfast, I wrapped a shawl around my shoulders to keep off the chill, and I wandered from here to there. The servants' quarters were below, of course, and I tiptoed past the kitchen, hoping not to disturb anyone. I opened doors and found empty rooms. One or two doors were locked. The downstairs was dark and dank—away from the kitchen—but not extraordinary. I followed the corridor outside to the barn and beyond. I walked past our smoldering fire ring toward the woods. The sun was bright today. It seemed our autumn had turned to fall again.

I noticed clumps of grass growing up in a small clearing to the north of the woods, so I walked toward it. I crouched down to move the grass away and was surprised to find two headstones.

One said, "Henry Blythe, cherished son." I could not discern the birth or death date. The other read, "Sarah Blythe, cherished daughter." Her dates were also obscure. I pulled away as much of the grass as I could. Then I went back to the house to find the gardener, so he could put right the little cemetery.

I passed Maryann as I started down the path toward the front of the house.

"Maryann, I've just found two gravestones for a Henry and Sarah Blythe. Do you know of them?"

"Aye," she said. "They were the children of the owner. They died in the pond out back one summer, both of them. It was tragic, madam. They think one of the children got a cramp so the other jumped in to help. Although no one knows for sure. They were both just found dead, floating on the surface. They had the pond drained soon after—that's why you haven't seen it. Then they sold the place."

"Thank you, Maryann," I said. "Could you please ask the gardener to cut down the weeds and make the plots tidy again?"

"Certainly, Mrs. Van Helsing."

As I walked back into the house, I wondered if Abraham had known about the deaths of these children. Had he kept this information from me? Such nonsense: to pretend the world is a pretty place does not mean it *will* then become a pretty place! That is not the Abraham I married.

3 Nov.—I could barely get out of bed this morning. The room was suffused with light. And something else. It was as if the walls breathed. No, that is not quite right. As if the walls panted. Like a mad dog from thirst. I called Maryann into the room, but she heard nothing.

"Is it not too bright in here?"

"Shall I close the draperies?" she asked.

I consented, but it did no good. My son Abraham came into the room then. He hesitated at the door and looked around.

"Mother," he said. "I don't like the wallpaper."

"Neither do I," I said. "Perhaps we can change it."

"What's behind it?" he asked.

I slowly got out of bed, relieved and terrified that Abraham sensed something in the room, too.

"I have wondered that very same thing," I said. I reached out for Abraham's hand. "It's too light in here. I can't see what's behind the paper. I think if the wallpaper were darker, I might be able to tell, don't you think?"

"I don't know, Mama."

At that moment I saw something move beneath the wallpaper—causing the wall to undulate, like leaves do when a snake or mole passes underneath them. Only this movement in the wall sent a chill of terror up my spine.

My son tugged on my hand, and we left the room.

I was certain then that the evil *had* followed me that day and was now lodged behind the wallpaper. I didn't know why. Had I been vulnerable, like someone is before they become ill with a cold? Was this house somehow vulnerable, too? Abraham would want me to know why, would want me to address it all scientifically. Why me? Why now? Why that wall? Perhaps so it could be with me as I slept, invade my dreams? I did not know why. I only knew I had to find a way to protect my son and husband from it. I had to make certain it did not touch our family—any more than it already had.

Abraham Van Helsing's Journal—

3 November.—I am glad to be finished with my work and am eager to rejoin my family. Dr. Ehrenreich and I performed trepanning on the patient. When he recovered his senses, he was quite rational, and his wife said she could see her husband in his

eyes again. "Seeing him in his eyes" was a strange utterance, yet I understood what she meant. He was sane again after the treatment. Unfortunately, he caught the meninge and died. His wife said, "I thank you for relieving his agony. At least he has died with the evil wrenched from his soul."

Her words reminded me of Catherine's. I was tempted to explain the science of her husband's disease but decided my neutral words were not what she needed to hear.

I can hardly bear to be away from my own beloved for so long. Tonight we will be together again!

4 November.—I should have never gone to London. I was completely fooled by Catherine's demeanor before I left. I fear she wanted me gone so she could indulge in her delusions. That sounds harsh, doesn't it? I do not mean it so. She cannot help herself. She is ill. But they were *dancing* in the moonlight! I suppose that is great sport for someone who is well, but she could have gotten a chill. And a fever would have exacerbated the wildness of her imagination.

Today she told me she wanted to change the wallpaper again.

"I cannot," I said. "We haven't the funds."

"But it is for my well-being," she said. "For your son's well-being."

"I would be indulging your fantasies," I said. "There is nothing wrong with the wallpaper."

"It needs to be darker," she said. "Or tear it down all together and paint the walls black. Then whatever is there will be gone." She stopped herself. She looked wild. "*Wait*. Oh! I had not thought of that! No, you must *not* take off the wallpaper. Cover it with more. We must keep it all inside."

"Catherine, you sound quite foolish," I said. "What has come over you?"

She turned to me. Her eyes looked feverish, and I felt afraid. Was it more than melancholy that taxed her? I remembered what my patient's wife had said about her husband not being in his eyes. Catherine was in hers. But she appeared quite agitated.

"I must tell you what has been happening," she said. "You must listen to every word and not judge until I am finished. Sit, husband."

I did as instructed. Catherine sat beside me.

"I was coming back from my work at the charity hospital. One of our cases had left the hospital suddenly—she had been severely beaten by one of her customers. I was concerned, so I got her address and instructed a cab driver to take me to it. He did not want to go—at least not with me. 'No place for a lady,' he said, and other such nonsense.

"But I convinced him," Catherine said. "He stopped in front of what looked to be a boarding house. It was quite rundown. The streets were full of people. Drunks, prostitutes, orphaned children, people going to and from work. Like any other place, I suppose, only more lively. It did not frighten me. I asked the driver to go up and see if he could find Mrs. Lansing. He left and—"

"He left you alone in the carriage?"

"Abraham, you must *listen*. I was alone in the cab. But I was safe. I watched the people. It was quite entertaining. And then I saw this man walking toward me. At least at first I thought he was a man. He looked like a man. Walked like a man. He had a black walking stick, I remember, and he swung it back and forth as he walked. He had a tall black top hat. A shiny gold waist coat. I was certain he was only walking toward the cab to walk beyond it. He did not look at me—until he was right next to the window. Then he turned to me without breaking stride and looked directly into my eyes. What I saw shook me to my very core. His eyes were not human, husband. They were not animal—I do not mean that. They were not those of a wild creature. Not like that. They were inhuman. Un-alive. I was filled with this awful sense of dread. As I tried to withdraw my gaze from his, he smiled. I wanted to scream but could not find my voice. In those instants, he took something from me. My vitality. Then he was gone. And I was shattered. I heard the next morning that those two women had been murdered. No man did that, Abraham. Evil did that."

"Men kill all the time, Catherine!"

She shook her head. "This was different. Evil exists. On its own. In a form that is not human. Is not animal. It just is, Abraham. It *took* from me, and I am afraid part of it has also latched onto me. And now it is here with us. And this evil—this thing—will steal from us. It will take what vitality I have left and crush it. It will steal what makes you my husband and Abraham my son. I believe we must leave this place, Abraham. And we must leave soon."

She was breathing heavily, almost panting.

I poured her a glass of water from the decanter on the table nearest me. Her hands shook as she took the water from me.

"I am not very strong," Catherine said, "and I feel as though I am getting weaker. This morning, before dawn, I awakened and I knew it was in the room with me. I felt this terrible weight on my chest. I could not move. I could not call to anyone to protect Abraham. I could only stare. After a while, I saw something behind the wallpaper. I was able to move then, and I got out of bed. With my hands, I felt around the entire room, looking for it. But it moves faster than I can. If I find it, I will smash it out of existence. But my strength fades, husband; it fades."

"You must calm yourself! Shall I give you something?"

"I have taken your pills, salts, and remedies," Catherine said. "I am not sick!"

"That feeling you had this morning," I said. "The weight on your chest. It is called a succubus dream, or an old hag dream.

They often occur when one is suffering from exhaustion. You have exhausted yourself with these fears, Catherine."

"Why didn't you tell me about the children drowning?"

"I-I. What children? Oh. I thought it might disturb you."

She laughed. An almost unnatural sound. "Of course it is disturbing and tragic, but so is life! We must look it in the face. Accept what is. Please, you must get us out of here."

"All right, my dear. I will try to arrange to change the lease."

Catherine shook her head. "Haven't you heard anything I've said?"

"Of course I have," I said. I took her hand in mine and squeezed it. "Don't sleep in your room tonight. Stay with me. Or I'll find you another room."

She nodded. "As you wish."

I am at the end of my wits! This morning Abraham started to come into Catherine's bed chamber, and she yelled at him to stay out. She ran down the hall after him, barely dressed, her hair flying every which way. She looked quite mad.

"You mustn't go near there," she said once she had caught up with him. "That is the heart of it. You must stay away until Father gets us away from here."

Catherine Van Helsing's Journal—

? Nov.—I am not sure what day it is. I write in the dark. I like the dark. I can see. Moonlight comes through the window and falls across this page. Moonlight is safe, too. It has a quiet, inner beauty. It knows. In this darkness, I can see the truth. Abraham is asleep. I left our bed and found the paint I arranged for the gardener to leave for me. He could not find black, but he poured color into color until he had almost black. It likes the brightness: the pretend brightness. Where we can pretend all is well. So I painted the wall black. Each time my paint brush touched the wallpaper, what was beneath seemed to undulate. Frantically, like a fish out of water. That made me happy. Each coat of paint is another wall I am erecting to keep the evil trapped here, unable to harm anyone else. Maybe then we can escape, leave it behind, and be safe.

The paint odor has made me quite dizzy, so now I sit by the open window. I was right, you know. The dark wallpaper allows me to see the wall as it truly is. And something is moving underneath the paper. Sometimes it is shapeless. Sometimes it has the shape of a human. A human who is not quite right. Nauseating in its distortion from normalcy.

Now it is whispering to me.

"Let me out," it says. "Let me out and you will be free."

It is a constant refrain now, in-between the panting. Is it right? Will I finally be free once it is released from these walls?

I shake my head. No, that is evil talking.

It must remain shackled.

But it won't stop whispering.

I fall to sleep.

When I awaken, I hear tapping. I listen carefully. It is as if someone is tapping their fingernails against something. Against the wallpaper—*from the inside!* It is testing the paper. Trying to find a weak point.

So it can tear the wall open and release itself!

I must do something!

Abraham Van Helsing's Journal—

5 November.—I awakened to the sound of something slamming against a wall. Then Catherine's scream. I jumped out of bed—first noticing that Catherine was not in the bed beside me. I ran toward the sound. My son cowered in the doorway to his mother's chamber, crying. Moonlight poured through the window. Catherine stood on the other side of the room heaving the back

of a shovel against the wall. She groaned with the effort every time the metal hit the wall.

"Catherine!" I cried, running to her.

"I struck it a couple of times," she said, nearly breathless. She smiled, then laughed. "It's not invincible. It even cried out when I hit it!"

She raised the shovel again, and I grabbed it from her. "That was you, Catherine! *You* were screaming!"

"It's here, Abraham. The evil is here, and it is trying to get out! To get at us. I must stop it!"

"You are acting insane!"

"Give the shovel back to me!"

I glanced at my son. He trembled in the darkness to see his mother thus.

"There is nothing here," I said. "This is all nonsense."

I raised the point of the shovel and drove it into the wall.

Catherine cried out. "No, you mustn't!"

I dropped the shovel and grabbed at the now torn wallpaper and began ripping it away from the wall. "See, there is nothing!"

Catherine ran to Abraham.

"Nothing!" I said. "It is just a wall with—"

And then something leaped out of the hole I had created—some *thing* I can't describe, sucking away all the air as it went by me. Then Catherine screamed, strangely, her voice broken and terrified. She pushed Abraham to the floor. I tried to run to them.

"No!" Catherine called. She reached out. She reached out . . . for it.

Put herself between us and it.

Then she screamed again.

Only it was no longer Catherine's voice, even though the sound emanated from her mouth.

I grabbed Abraham and pulled him up against me.

Catherine collapsed to the floor, gurgling, laughing.

Maryann was suddenly at the door holding up a lantern. The light made the shadows sharper. When Catherine looked up at her, Maryann gasped. I put my hand over Abraham's eyes.

Catherine turned to me, and I was filled with a dread I cannot explain. I knew in that moment that my wife had saved us but was now lost herself. She was no longer in her eyes.

The instant I realized this, Catherine smiled.

"Get the doctor," I told Maryann.

I led Abraham around and away from his mother—my back against the wallpaper and Abraham's back against me—until we were out of the room. I heard Catherine get up, heard the sound of tearing as she pulled the black paper from the walls, heard her panting.

"It's free now, eh husband!" She screamed, then laughed. "Now you know you should have listened to her! You'll be next. She never loved you, you pompous man! She felt trapped by you and your life!"

I pulled the door shut and took my latch key from my pocket. My son watched as my shaking hand put the key in the lock and turned it.

"What has happened to Mama?" Abraham asked.

"She has left us to save us," I said as we walked quickly down the corridor toward the front door. "When you are older, I will tell you the whole story. She has saved us this night."

I began to weep. The thing in the bedroom continued to cackle and rip paper. Would I tell Abraham my part in his mother's demise?

"You should have listened!" she screamed, the sound of her voice getting more and more distant.

"My beloved," I whispered.

I tightened my grip on her son's hand. "You already know of your mother's sweetness and loving care. But you should also know that your mother was a brave and gallant woman, and all who knew her loved her well!"

Except one.

I had not loved her well enough.

But I would make it up to her.

I swear to you, sweet Catherine. I will make it up to you! I will show people the truth. I will stare evil in the face—and I shall be the victor. This I promise you, my beloved wife.

And just then, as we were about to step outside, the voice that had been Catherine's came to us clearly by some trick of acoustics. She whispered, "Let me out, and you will be finally free."

Ghost Writer

"OK. This DEA agent is taking a cruise on an ocean liner when he discovers a body in one of the dining rooms, and a bunch of drug dealers take over the ship."

The famous writer we will call Carl Harding shook his head. "No, I told you I'm sick of all that action crap I write. I want something more thoughtful."

Samantha flipped through the index cards in her little black box. So far she had suggested ten story ideas for him, and he had not liked any of them.

"Here's one. A woman and man on the brink of divorce win a trip to Provence. As they drive through the French countryside, they begin to reconnect. Then they have a car accident and one of them is going to die, so the other one donates blood or a kidney or something."

"That's a little too thoughtful," Mr. Harding said. "And I don't like hospital stuff." He leaned back in his chair and glanced around Samantha's studio apartment. "I don't think there's anything in that little black box for me. Too bad. I'd heard you're a great ghost—especially surprising since you're so young. You've supplied story ideas to the very best of us old farts who've run out of ideas, or so I've been told."

"You aren't old," Samantha said, by rote. "You're just too busy to come up with the actual ideas." She smiled and continued looking through the box. "Technically, though, I don't think I'm a ghost writer—you do the writing, I just come up with the ideas. I'm not that young. I'm nearly twenty-two."

Mr. Harding smiled, then said, "Speaking of ghosts: How about a ghost story? I don't think I've ever written a ghost story."

"OK. Here's one I've never shown anyone else. And it's got a ghost. You want to hear it?"

"Sure. I came all this way."

Samantha looked at the card for a moment and then said, "So this family has just moved to a farm, let's say in southern Ohio. Maybe they inherited the land. It was the mother's mother who owned it. Been in the family for generations although this family hadn't spent a lot of time there before. They had lived in Michigan. Mother worked for a law firm in Detroit, father is a writer. A somewhat successful writer."

"I don't know. I don't like writing about writers."

"Hear me out," Samantha said. "It makes a difference to the story."

The famous writer we will call Mr. Harding shrugged.

"They're on holiday at Lake Michigan where they go all the time. Benton Harbor or someplace like that. You could find a spot on the map. They have three children. Thomas, an older teenage boy, seventeen, eighteen; Cynthia, she's maybe fifteen, and Emily, she's about twelve. Emily is sweet and kind. Cynthia is a smart-ass—it's her defense when she's afraid, nervous, uncomfortable. Her parents tell her that her mouth is going to get her in trouble one day if she doesn't learn to control it. Teachers are always getting pissed at her. She loses friends because of her sharp tongue. She tries to keep her mouth shut, but she feels like she's telling the truth, and what could be wrong with that? Thomas picks on the girls. He's a bully. The parents don't see it. He's a football hero at school and nice around them. They don't see him always making sexually inappropriate remarks to Cynthia."

"Yeah, yeah, I got it, typical teenage boy."

Samantha frowned. "Just so you know: It doesn't feel typical to girls. Being teased that way. At least for the story."

He waved to her to go on. "I don't normally like stories with children in them. Are you getting to the ghost?"

"Mr. Harding, it's a short story, not flash fiction. It'll take a minute or two."

"Sorry, go ahead."

"So they're by Lake Michigan. The parents are up the beach or in their cottage. Thomas is supposed to be out with friends, but he's stopped on his way to tease his sisters. Emily is playing in the sand. Cynthia is running in and out of the waves. Lake Michigan can have huge waves, and on this day, they are amazing. Cynthia is in a new bathing suit and feels awkward, especially since her brother keeps saying things like, 'Are those bee stings or breasts?' loud enough for the whole beach to hear except no one can really hear anything over the sound of the waves. Thomas follows Cynthia as she runs in and out of the waves, taunting her. Finally as the wave goes out, Cynthia stands her ground and screams at her brother to leave her alone. She's in tears by now. Thomas starts calling her a cry baby. Furious and frustrated because she's had to live with Thomas's bullying for so long, she reaches out and pushes her brother. She's smaller than he is, but he loses his balance on the wet sand and falls just as the wave comes back in. He laughs as he falls. 'You are so dead, sister,' he yells. Then the wave covers him, and he disappears. Cynthia waits for him to pop back up. But he doesn't. The wave goes out and comes back: without Thomas. She screams in horror for her parents.

"The next time we see the family, they're at the farm. The

mother has quit her job, and they've all moved out to this country farmhouse. It's beautiful land. Lush, rich with huge old oak and maple trees. The parents didn't want to be around any water, but there is an old mill, barn, and stream at the far end of the land which they tell the girls to avoid. The parents are depressed over Thomas's death, quiet; they don't pay much attention to the girls. It's near the end of the summer. The girls are outside exploring most of the time, and what they are drawn to is, of course, the old mill, barn, and stream.

"Cynthia remembers when she was younger her grandmother telling her that a milkmaid supposedly haunted the barn. She remembers going to the barn with her father when she was a little girl and asking him if he wanted to write a story about the milkmaid. Her father said he couldn't think of a story for the milkmaid. 'Maybe if you ask her,' Cynthia said. Her father had laughed. Thomas, who had gone with them to the barn, had rolled his eyes. 'You can't talk to ghosts, you idiot,' he said. 'Then you come up with a story,' Cynthia told her older brother. 'Maybe I will,' he said. 'And it'll be better than anything you or Dad could come up with.' 'Well, son, it's one thing to come up with story ideas. It's quite another to sell them.' 'I could do it,' Thomas said. 'I'd make us rich.' Her father had nodded. 'I'm sure you could, son.' Her parents believed Thomas could do anything.

"Emily and Cynthia like hanging out at the stream and barn. It's lush and green and fairyland-like. You could describe it well, Mr. Harding. You've always been good with description. This place could look like something out of a fairy tale book. One day as dusk is falling and the girls need to get home for dinner, they run through the old barn one more time, laughing and play-ing tag, and the air suddenly shimmers and lights up, as though a shaft of moonlight has made its way into the room, and then a milky white woman begins to take shape. She motions to them to come closer and seems to want to tell them something, but they scream and run away.

"'She was so beautiful,' Emily tells her sister as they lay in bed trying to sleep that night. 'I want to go back and see her. She couldn't hurt us, could she? Ghosts are good, aren't they?'

"Cynthia doesn't know whether ghosts are good or not, but she finally says she'll go back with Emily. She can't sleep. She thinks about her brother. Ghosts are dead people, right, she thinks? Well, her brother Thomas was dead, and he wasn't exactly good people. He teased her so much. Plus he used to sneak into her room at night and do things to her she had not liked when he was alive. Told her if she ever told anyone, he'd do it to Emily, too. So she had kept her mouth shut and had kept Emily close to her side. Thomas had left Emily alone, but Cynthia had noticed him eying her that summer, the summer he died, and Cynthia hadn't known what to do. Truth be told, she had been relieved when he drowned. And horrified. Now when her parents looked at her, she could see that they blamed her. She wanted to tell them what a terrible boy Thomas had been, but she knew they wouldn't believe her. What if the milkmaid had been a bad person in real life, too? Did that mean she would be a bad ghost? Did it mean she could hurt them? Cynthia finally decided she had never heard of a ghost actually hurting anyone.

"So the next day the girls go back to the barn. They don't see anything. All seems normal. They play hide and seek amongst the huge old trees. Around dusk, they return to the barn. The air seems to shift, moonlight fills the barn from an unknown source, and the milkmaid shimmers into view. The sisters clutch each other to keep from running while they watch the beautiful woman. She wants them to come closer. And she is trying to say something. She looks frustrated that they can't hear her.

"'Can you turn up your speaker?' Cynthia asks. Emily elbows her. 'Sorry,' Cynthia says. But it is too late. The milkmaid disappears. The girls go home, trying to figure out what they can do so they can hear the ghost. Emily looks on the calendar and sees that the next night is full moon. 'I bet we can hear her then,' Emily says. 'Full moon is supposed to be a magical time.' Cynthia dreams that night that her brother comes into her room and puts his hand over her mouth, just like he used to when he was alive. She does not want to go to the barn the next day, but Emily convinces her everything will be all right. At dusk, they go into the barn and sit on the old dusty floorboards, waiting. And sure enough, as the moon rises, the milkmaid comes into view.

""'Is there something you want to tell us?' Emily asks. Cynthia is amazed that Emily is not afraid. She never seems afraid of anything. Cynthia is shaking. She is afraid she is going to say something stupid—ordinarily, the more nervous she got, the more smartass her mouth got.

"The milkmaid opens her mouth to speak and this time the girls can hear the words. 'I am Mary, the milkmaid,' the ghost says. 'I have haunted this barn for many decades waiting for someone to hear my story. I used to work for a rich couple who owned this farm. Every morning they forced me to milk their cows and bring them milk to drink. They told me I was not allowed to ever drink the milk. One day, I was very thirsty. So I had only a sip. I didn't realize that the cow was ill. I got milk fever and died the next day.'

""'Is that it?' Cynthia asks. 'Is that your entire story? That is a really stupid story.' Emily nudges her sister. 'I liked it,' Emily says. The air in the barn is now doing something more than shimmering. It is vibrating. And the milkmaid is changing, pulsing, shapeshifting in horrible ways. Suddenly she is a monster, reaching out for the girls. She snatches up Emily and tosses her through the open barn door and into a huge old oak. Cynthia screams as her sister hits the oak tree and disappears into it. She runs to the tree. A ghostly white shape appears on the tree trunk—a shape that resembles Emily.

"Cynthia turns around, and the white shimmering light has followed her, only it is no longer a monster or the milkmaid. Her brother stands before her, his arms crossed.

"'Mom and Dad always said your mouth would get you into trouble,' he says. 'You think you could tell a better story? You always thought you were better than me.'

"'Where's Emily? Thomas, you promised you wouldn't hurt her.'

"'That was then,' he says. 'But I haven't harmed her. You have. She is inside that old oak, trapped. I can let her out, though. And I will, Miss Smartass. You think you're a better story teller than I am? Dad always said it wasn't the idea that counted, it was if you could sell it or not. So you can have Emily back as soon as you sell one hundred stories. I'll make it easy on you: I'll give Emily back if you sell one hundred story *ideas* or stories. Whichever. Think of yourself as a modern Scheherazade telling tales to keep your sister alive, instead of yourself. Only I'm a good guy and won't make you tell 1,001 tales.'

"'Thomas! You can't do this to Emily. You can't do this to Mom and Dad. They're so sad that you're dead.'

"'And whose fault is that?' He shimmers and pulsates and becomes the monster again, hissing and screaming at her. 'Hurry up before I change my mind!' he roars.

"And so Cynthia runs back to the house and tells her parents what has happened. No one believes her. The police come. They take her away, believing she has harmed her sister. Of course they never find Emily's body. Cynthia is sent back to her parents, who don't want her. Meanwhile she is writing stories like crazy, but she can't get anyone to buy them. She is too young, she doesn't really know much about writing. So she starts just coming up with ideas. She sells a couple to her father, then he quits writing.

So she starts asking his friends if they want any ideas. And they buy some."

Samantha paused and took a drink of water from the glass next to her.

"So what happened?" Mr. Harding asked. "Did she ever sell one hundred stories?"

"What do you think? You could end it whatever way you want. Maybe her parents divorced. Her mother wanted to sell the farm, but Cynthia convinced her not to—just in case her sister returned. Or maybe she wasn't able to convince her mother, and the farm has been sold, and the new owners are going to clear-cut the land in ten days, so she's got ten days to finish selling her stories. She could be up to 95. Only five more to go—except it has taken her *years* to sell that many. Maybe you'll want her to succeed when you write it. Let's say she sells her hundred stories, and she goes back to the deserted farm and calls her brother and shows him that she has sold a hundred story ideas, and he releases her sister. As Emily comes out of the tree, time goes backwards, so that no time has passed at all, and they are two young girls again looking for ghosts in their grandmother's barn. They live happily ever after. It could happen."

Mr. Harding sat up. "I like that one. I'll buy it. I'll probably have to leave out the molestation part, since I've sold it to a men's magazine."

"Why? Because they're all a bunch of perverts, too?" Samantha asked. She cringed. She had to learn to keep her mouth shut.

"Yes, well, I've got to make a living, and they've already shelled out a nice chunk of change for this piece on spec. They just want my name, don't care what I'm writing. It's a tough way to make a living, this writing thing."

"Yep, even when it's life or death."

Mr. Harding nodded. "Even when it's life or death. Should I make the check out to you?"

Samantha nodded. "And send me a copy of the story once it's published, if you don't mind. I like keeping them for my files. Let your friends know I'm available. I've got some bills coming due soon, so I can use the money. Is it ever life or death for you, Mr. Harding?"

Mr. Harding handed her the check. She gave him the index card.

"Life or death? Hmmmm. I've got a kid in college, a house payment due, and my wife was just laid off. Let's just say it's pretty necessary. Thank you. I'll be back if I need more ideas."

"Thanks," Samantha called as he went out her door.

She looked down at her black box.

"OK, Emily. That's ninety-six. I'm coming, honey. I promise. I'm coming soon."

She glanced over at the empty corner of her apartment. That's where Thomas usually showed up, his arms folded, watching her, taunting her, asking her how many more she had to go before she got to one hundred. She wished he was still alive, even if it meant he had kept coming into her room. At least then she could have protected Emily from him. From this. From her.

Samantha stood, reached for her jacket, and put it on. She had heard that a writer's group met at the pub down the street every Tuesday night. It was Tuesday. Maybe she would find some poor slob who was desperate for a story idea. She had ten days to go and four more story ideas to sell.

"You can do it," she told herself. "I'm coming, little sister. I'm coming."

Desire

Oct 10, 1994

Should I begin this with Dear Diary? I haven't kept a journal since I was a girl of twelve. It feels silly, yet essential now. I am here, on the Oregon coast, living in the old lighthouse keeper's house. My first day. Millie, the caretaker, has left for her vacation after she assured me the house isn't haunted, despite the rumors.

"I've lived here four years and never heard a thing!" she said, giggling. Strange to see a grown woman giggle. She waved, got into her Volkswagen and drove away, leaving me with a spectacular view of the cove, the Pacific, and the deep dark black-green forest that surrounds three sides of the keeper's house. From here I can't see the lighthouse that the Coast Guard still uses.

Inside the house, all is quiet and empty. Like me? Some metaphor for my life. Ah, I can't start feeling sorry for myself yet. I only just got here. And it was my idea. I have dreamed of this house for so long; it was time I came.

They all think I'm doing research on lighthouses and the women living in them in the nineteenth century.

But I am here to meet the ghosts. They have been calling to me all my life.

Oct 12, 1994

I slept through the entire night, can't remember dreaming. I had to put the cat in the other part of the house—this house is really two residences. The lighthouse keeper and his family shared the structure with his assistant and his family. The two huge twin apartments are separated by a door. The southern apartment is empty; the northern is empty except for the few rooms Millie uses: bathroom, kitchen, library, bedroom. The cat is not happy, but I'm allergic to cats. I waved to her through the beveled glass in the separating door. She promptly ran outside and tried to come in the back door. It's not going to be a pleasant three weeks for her.

Sorry, kitty.

It's mid-afternoon now, and I'm sitting outside on the porch. The cat sleeps at my feet. Apparently I am forgiven. The house is so quiet. I came here for a rest, for silence, to be away from all the horrors of the world, yet inside the house I am disturbed by the quiet. I played the radio yesterday and all morning.

The ghosts haven't shown themselves, if they exist at all.

It has been years since I heard one of them speak; maybe I imagined them. Maybe I was "touched" only when I was a child, and now it's gone.

Mercy, I'm tired.

I haven't heard my own voice in 24 hours. Actually, I'm not certain I've ever really heard my own voice.

Oct 13, 1994

I dreamed I was stuck in an elevator. I couldn't get out, so I graded student papers. I was completely resigned to the fact that I was stuck in that stupid elevator.

For breakfast I cooked pancakes, potatoes, eggs, and sausage.

Yes, me, the vegetarian. I let the cat in and fed her the sausage. She loved it.

Outside, wind strokes the house. The ocean laps on the beach below. I cannot see the parking lot or the path that leads up to the house; for that I am grateful. So far I've only seen a few tourists. They've all heeded the "no admittance" sign, however, and haven't tried to get into the house. The president of the Historical Society—they own the house—called to see how I was doing. I hated hearing my voice. I like the silence. The house creaks all around me. As yet, I have not walked up to the lighthouse.

Oct 14, 1994

I heard fireworks. As if it were the Fourth of July. They woke me. I went out, stood on the porch, and saw nothing. I heard them exploding all about me. And the lawn was silvered as if with moon light, yet it was new moon.

I think the ghosts have finally talked to me. I am still touched.

When I was a girl, ghosts always talked to me. I could walk into any place and hear conversations where there were no people; sometimes I saw people where there were no people. My mother took me to the doctor who said I was probably schizophrenic. My mother and father wept night after night. Until I went to the home of people I had never known and an Aunt Betsy, who wasn't really there, leaned over to me and said, "Tell my cousin Charlotte that I left the pearls under the floorboard in the back closet." I said it out loud. The woman Charlotte screamed and ran to her closet. She came back with a necklace of pearls, fake pearls, but pearls nonetheless. My parents took me to a priest next for an exorcism. He told them to leave me alone. I was just a troubled child in a troubled world. He winked at me as I left. I listened to the ghosts for a few years after that, trying to see if any of the chatter had anything to do with me. It didn't. Gradually, I stopped listening, until I no longer heard.

I grew up. Worked too hard. Got married. Divorced. Separated—from myself. Funny hearing Millie giggle. As if she had done something wrong. It wasn't that. It's just that I've forgotten how to laugh. I've been feeling too tired and sick for so long.

I had to put the cat out again. She left me wheezing. I vacuumed the entire house. That left me exhausted. Hopefully I got all the cat hair and didn't vacuum up any spirits.

Oct 16, 1994

Before I went to bed, I looked through the beveled glass of the adjoining door to say good night to the cat. She was nowhere in sight. On the other side of the stairs, however, someone stood in the parlor. A woman, dressed in white. I wasn't frightened. Only mildly curious. The ghosts had asked me to come to this house, hadn't they? Interrupting my dreams for months. Now I was here. I opened the door and slipped into the southern apartment. I tiptoed in the darkness across the foyer, past the stairs, to stand at the entrance of the parlor. I stared at the woman.

She looked so real. Her reddish brown hair was piled on top of her head, just barely: Most of it was trying to fall down. She held something in her hand which I could not see. That wasn't unusual. I remembered when I was a child that I would often see only parts of things, people, places. A tableau with missing pieces. She tipped her hand and drank whatever I could not see. Her eyes were green, her cheeks flushed red. I could almost taste what touched her lips—dry white wine. Her dress went up her pretty neck, touching her chin, and down to her shoes. She was trying to dress up, yet she appeared disheveled. She was not made for the parlor. I could see her running outside amongst the trees. In the forest.

The forest where I never went.

She turned to me but did not see me. She smiled at some secret thought and I stared at her face. Yes, this was why I was here. This woman. I knew her. Had known her long ago. And she took my breath away.

The cat meowed. I looked down as she rubbed my legs. When I looked up again, the woman was gone.

Bridget. That was her name. I was certain of it.

Oct 17, 1994

I could hardly sleep. All I could think of was Bridget. How did I know her? Who was she? I twisted and turned and finally fell to sleep.

This morning I feel strangely rested. I think I'll take a walk up to the lighthouse.

The path to the lighthouse is almost overgrown. They keep it clear enough for the Coast Guard to service the now-automatic light. For a while, as I walk along the path, the wind is blocked, and I hear the distant roar of the ocean. Close by, birds call to one another, and to me, I suppose. I look to either side and the forest grows black-green and seemingly silent, until I stand still and listen. Life flourishes all around me. Ferns reach out to stroke my hands as I pass by. Briars are heavy with blackberries. I lean to pluck them from the vine, and then I hesitate. Maybe these berries have been sprayed; they would not be safe. I want them, yet I don't want to risk an allergic reaction.

I sigh and continue my walk. When did everything become so unsafe? As if the world is shot to hell and we're all left standing, battered, bruised, possibly dead, and we just don't know enough to fall down. Not "we." Me. Me. I'm tired of being the walking wounded. I'm tired of trying to figure out what is wrong with me. No doctor seems to know for certain. No therapist can untwist my inner being. I am exhausted by the struggle.

Ahead of me, the forest opens to green grass. The lighthouse beacon revolves in the autumn sunlight. Behind me the forest sings; beyond, the ocean rolls against the sand. I sigh and sink to the earth. Mother, I'm tired of trying so hard. Of being so sick.

I slept. Out under the sun, the ocean my lullaby. When I awakened, Bridget lay on the grass near me. She stared up at the sky. Her hair lay in a halo all around her, red and curly. Her dress was loose, exposing her neck and part of her chest. She was singing, but I could not hear the words. She looked more real than she had last night.

"Bridget?" I said.

She continued to sing quietly. She stopped suddenly and sat up. I followed her gaze. Coming down the path was another woman, dressed in black, a parasol shielding her head from the sun. She was pale, her hair black and pulled completely away from her face. She smiled slightly when she saw Bridget, mouthing her name, but her face remained lined with grief. I knew this woman. Her name was Suzanne.

Bridget ran to her and flung her arms around her neck. Suzanne dropped her parasol and gently embraced Bridget. Suzanne was slight, or appeared to be, bound by her grief and the corset she wore. It seemed she could hardly breathe. She reminded me of myself. What a contrast she was to Bridget, whose waist was not cinched, her hair flowing across her bare shoulders.

"Sister!" Bridget whispered.

I could hear them!

Suzanne pulled away from Bridget. "I am glad to finally be here, but I am tired. Your brother doesn't like to stop to rest, and I am reluctant to ask."

"He is stupid," Bridget said affectionately, linking arms with Suzanne. "Let me take you back to the house. I didn't expect you this soon, though I am glad to have you. I have been alone for weeks."

"And they let you stay alone?" The two women turned to

walk down the path again. "I am surprised, though I shouldn't be. You have always been able to do as you please. It is your burning desire to be thoroughly free."

"My Annie, Suzannie," Bridget whispered. "I have never heard such tiredness as I hear in your voice. I will take care of you."

I jumped up to follow them, but when I reached the head of the path, the forest had swallowed their spirits.

I went back to the keeper's house. I looked through both apartments for the ghosts and found only a lonely cat. I went back to the northern house and turned on the radio. I found a station that played sad songs, and I turned up the volume while I made cookies. The cat stood on the windowsill outside watching while I kneaded dough. I thought of Bridget. How alive she seemed, even though she had been dead a hundred years or so. More alive than myself. When she moved, the forest moved with her. When she moved, she was in her body. I bet she loved her body. Loved the feel of it. Made love to herself and enjoyed others making love to her.

I couldn't even remember the last time I had had sex: alone or with a partner. I hadn't expected marriage and had been equally surprised by the divorce. Now relationships seemed too frightening, or something. All that passion, on the part of the other person, and then there was me. I always felt as though I was on the outside looking in. Except for a few years between the ages of seventeen and nineteen. I had been very sexual then, before the world knew about AIDS. Then, and for a few years after, I was happy and unafraid.

And then what?

I shaped the dough into cookies and put them in the oven. Then I had started getting sick: allergies, sinus infections, depression. I looked at the world and did not like what I saw.

I guess one could say I withdrew.

Just let me get through this life and move on to the next.

Jesus. That is pathetic. When did I become this depressed and depressing woman? 40 something and I'm ready for the scrap heap?

I burned the cookies and started to cry. I cried until my eyes swelled and I got sick to my stomach. Then I threw up the burned cookies. All in all, a stellar evening. No wonder I don't date much.

OCT 18, 1994

I awaken near three and go down into the parlor of the south apartment. Bridget sits next to Suzanne, who looks ill. I kneel in the entrance and watch. A man stands with them. His features mimic Bridget's, yet he is older, without her sense of humor, dressed in a military uniform of some sort. Ah, he must be the brother, the new lighthouse keeper? His arm is across the mantel as he talks to the women. Bridget rolls her eyes and smiles at Suzanne. Suzanne hides a smile.

"Brother, can't you see your wife is tired?" Bridget says.

"Bridget—" Suzanne begins.

"I'm sorry, but he cannot expect you to run this huge house by yourself in your condition."

"What do you mean?" brother says. "In what condition? My wife is no longer with child, I thought you knew."

Suzanne gasps and quickly gets up and leaves the room. I hear the swish of her skirts. The air moves as she runs past me and up the stairs.

"Benjamin Kelly," Bridget says, standing with her hands on her hips. "You are an insensitive idiot. Your assistant and his family will not be here for another two months. Hire someone from the village to help here. In the past year, your wife has administered to the wounds of soldiers, lost a child, and moved from her childhood home all the way across the country. Give her time!"

And then, suddenly, they are all gone. I am alone, sleepy, and ready for my own dreams.

Oct 19, 1994

Today is beautiful. The sky is clear except for some strategically placed clouds which take the glare off the ocean. I sit on the grass near the house and bathe in the sun and the sea air. Both feel like gentle strokes of someone's hands.

Near to me, Bridget and Suzanne lounge. Suzanne does not look quite as ill. Today she is dressed in blue. The parasol shades only part of her face. I brush my hair and watch as Bridget gets up to stand behind Suzanne. She takes down Suzanne's long black hair and begins to gently braid it. She whispers as she braids; I can almost feel Suzanne's hair in my hands. The ocean wind takes the sound of their voices away. Suzanne's face is relaxing. Tears slowly stream down her face; she smiles as if she doesn't know they are there. Beyond them, Benjamin gives orders to a stable boy. I see stables where before I only saw rundown garages.

Their world has become my world. I have unplugged the phone. Occasional tourists walk by, but I ignore them, and they don't seem to see me. Perhaps I really have slipped into the other time.

It is all right with me.

I want to be near Bridget.

Later, I am inside, sitting at the entrance to the parlor. Bridget is there, her hair up again, as she feigns propriety. Suzanne, her face still lined, sits near Benjamin, who stands at the mantel. Occasionally, Suzanne touches her breasts, as if in pain. Gradually, another man appears. His hair is longer than Benjamin's, a bit grayer, wilder, his beard long and untidy, a big man who fills the room with his laughter and voice. I smile. Bridget likes him; she has heard his stories before but listens with pleasure.

She glances at Suzanne, who smiles at the new man. Dobson, Bridget calls him.

"Mr. Dobson will visit us every few months," Bridget says. "Sometimes with his crew, sometimes not. He brings us our supplies."

"I have heard you are a fine tender," Benjamin says. "A fine tender!" Benjamin tries to be jovial, but he doesn't have the spirit for it.

The scene shifts as the cat rubs my legs. I lean down to pet her. "You're always spoiling the good parts," I whisper.

Oct 21, 1994

I went up into the woods today. Barefoot. Yes, I did. My feet hurt, yet it was glorious to dig my toes into the humus. I felt like the Goddess Diana running through the forest, crying for my hounds. I stopped at the briar patch and plucked ripe succulent blackberries and dropped them into my mouth. My body liked it all. Listen to me, talking about my body as if it were separate from me. *I* liked it.

When I came out of the woods, I nearly stumbled over Bridget and Dobson, walking arm and arm. She rested her head on his shoulder as they walked and he squeezed her waist.

"Where is that brother of yours?" Dobson asked.

"He's at the lighthouse, shining up the brass. He'll be gone all day."

"And your sister-in-law?"

"She's asleep, poor thing. She lost a child less than a month ago. Her heart and body still ache for the child."

Dobson took Bridget's hand and pulled her toward the stable.

"I don't want to hear about anyone but you, lass," he said. I ran to follow. "I've missed ye these past months!"

Bridget laughed and followed him into the stable. She backed into a wall and pulled Dobson toward her. They started kissing. She pulled at his shirt, he stroked her breasts. I went closer. She was breathing heavily, laughing, murmuring. She lifted her dress. My breathing quickened. She moved toward him, he pushed into her. I gasped and fell to my knees. I could feel him in me. Could feel her. Moving together. Moving. Finding pleasure. I could feel the wood against my back, Dobson inside Bridget, me. He knew how to please her. They cried out, shuddering and pushing together. An orgasm moved up through me, out my hands, feet, and head. They disappeared, and I was left alone lying in the grass, in plain view of anyone who cared to see, quivering with orgasm. I curled up on the grass, luxuriating in the feel of it, rubbing it against me. I didn't care if anyone saw. It was about time the world saw the face of a happy woman or two.

Oct 22, 1994

1 felt silly and blissful all day. Bridget. She was amazing. She had called me to this place to remember her. Remember how much I loved her. Remember how I had loved her body.

I had loved my own body at one time, I suppose. I must have. We come into this world all love. But something happened. It is sometimes difficult to remain loving and clear and strong in the face of so much—I'm not certain there's a word for it—so much hatred? We are not held in high esteem in this world. I thought I'd fix that by teaching women studies courses, making certain young women were strong and able, able to see themselves as whole beings. I always told my students to connect with other women, yet I had neglected to do that myself. It had seemed safer just to work, write, and be by myself.

Now I'm not certain I was even with myself. I was totally alone. Disconnected from others *and* myself.

I need to find that connectedness again.

I think the orgasm helped a bit with that.

I am giggling as I write this.

Oct 23, 1994

Suzanne sits in a huge bathtub while Bridget pours steaming water over her. She is a small pale woman except for her breasts; they look heavy, almost distorted. She cradles them gently.

Bridget sits on the floor behind Suzanne and begins brushing Suzanne's hair. The morning sunlight christens the room gold.

"You should never have married my brother," Bridget says.

"Don't say that," Suzanne says. "I have known him all my life. He is a good friend."

"You married him because you were tired," Bridget says.

Suzanne nods and looks at her breasts. "It is true. The hunger strikes exhausted me."

"Did you think that would really get women the vote?"

Suzanne nods again. "Yes. It will happen. Women are dying so that it will happen. And then the war." She stops.

"I know, sister, I know."

"You don't know what I saw." Her eyes fill with tears. My chest hurts. "They were just boys. Blood soaking into the Earth. We had to beg the doctors to get them to let us help."

"Maybe if women didn't help men during war, there would be no war," Bridget says.

Suzanne stiffens and blinks away her tears. "Do you really think so?"

"No, no, I'm sorry. If you hadn't helped, more boys would have died; that is the only difference it would have made."

"Now it's over, and I wanted to have child after child, to make up for the ones who died. Their body parts were scattered all over those hospitals. Legs here. Arms there. Do you think—do you wonder how their souls ever survived? Did they leave parts of their souls with those lost limbs? We're all so scattered."

Even back then? I feel scattered every day. Pieces of me littering the path I've taken.

"It hasn't always been like that," Bridget says. "It will not always be that way."

"Truly? The child that grew within me couldn't stay. My grief killed her. She could not bear it, so she let go of me. I killed my own dearest child."

She weeps openly now; Bridget strokes her hair and keens quietly.

After a time, Suzanne stands. The water drips from her naked body. Bridget gets a towel and gently helps her out of the tub. Neither woman seems embarrassed by Suzanne's nakedness. She drapes the towel over a chair and sits on it.

"My breasts ache so for my child," Suzanne says, her voice choked with tears. "I cannot let her go, buried in the Earth though she may be; my breasts long for her mouth." The grief lines her face again. She will be scarred for life by all that she has seen.

Bridget kneels at Suzanne's feet. Her hair is spread across her bare white shoulders. The sun shines through her night dress, silhouetting her body. She cups Suzanne's breast in her hand, leans forward, and puts her lips around her dark nipple. Suzanne strokes Bridget's hair, leans back and weeps silently as the other woman suckles her. I taste the liquid, mother's milk, sweet and bitter at the same time, like nothing I have ever tasted or felt, except maybe like the humus under my bare feet. Tears stream down Bridget's face and into her mouth, mingling with Suzanne's milk. I close my eyes and weep out loud.

I wander from house to house. Outside it rains. The cat follows me, imitating my restlessness. I have loved Bridget forever, I know that now.

I am desperate to see her again, but the house remains empty save for myself and the cat. We turn on the radio and dance to strange music. I dance; the cat watches. I twirl around the empty house and laugh at the cat watching me. My laughter reminds me of Bridget.

I go into the modern bathroom and take a long bath. When I get out, I dry myself and then walk from room to room, naked. How wonderful to feel the air against my skin. I put a blanket down in the middle of the empty parlor and give myself a massage. I don't know if I have ever before touched every part of my body. I like the feel of my own butt, my breasts, even the flabby skin on my arms. The cat licks herself.

I get up, tingly from my massage, and dance naked around the parlor.

I find Bridget and Suzanne in my bed. Suzanne's black hair is spread out behind her. Black and gorgeous. Hair everywhere. Bridget's red curly hair. They hug and squeeze their breasts together. Suzanne flinches slightly and Bridget leans over and kisses Suzanne's breasts, one at a time, her tongue lingering on one, her hand moving up Suzanne's thigh. I am next to them, feeling their hands on me as they stroke each other, feeling their orgasms as they move against one another, arms and legs twined around the other, their skin like beacons in my dark room. Contentedly, I fall asleep beside them.

Oct ? 1994

I have followed them for days. Or they me. I watch them squat on the Earth, naked, running from house to house, loving each other, pretending not to when others are around. The grief falls away from Suzanne. She becomes beautiful with love. Even Benjamin seems to relax. Flowers fill the parlor, kitchen, and bedrooms. Briars crawl up the sides of the house. The women wear their hair down, their feet bare. At night, they play in the ocean.

I am with them. A ghost to the ghosts. I am glad Bridget had a great love, was loved by a woman like Suzanne. And vice versa.

When Bridget laughs, the world shifts. Things change. I love them both, but Bridget is who I have always wanted to be.

In just a few days, I will have to go home and leave them behind.

Oct 31,1994

The cat and I decorated the house for Halloween. My favorite holiday. It has been decades since I celebrated. How could I have forgotten how fun it was? I dressed in a long silvery dress of Millie's. The cat tried to eat pumpkin seeds and quickly spat them out. I laughed at her; my laughter filled the house and my body, and the world seemed to change.

The entire house transforms as we put the Jack-o-Lantern out on the porch. I notice for the first time that the cat sees the ghosts, too. She watches now as they flit to and fro, dressed in costumes of one sort or another. Did they invite some of the villagers in for a party?

Suzanne is more beautiful than I have ever seen her, clothed in a purple low-cut dress, a purple mask over her eyes. She dances with Benjamin and he whispers in her ear. Dobson is there, bellowing and flirting with every woman near him. When Bridget enters the room, everyone stops, for a moment, because she is so beautiful. She is the fairy queen, dressed in a green dress that matches the design of Suzanne's. Her mask is green, too, darker than her eyes, highlighting her long red hair. She carries a wand in one hand.

Tomorrow I leave this place. Tomorrow I leave Bridget.

I go upstairs to an empty room and sit on the floor. I came to this house sick and depressed. I have learned to feel again, to rejoice in my body, the land, all that is around me. I am myself again. The cat licks my hand and I start to cry.

"Who is that keening as if there be no tomorrow?"

I look up. Bridget stands in the doorway looking down at me. She holds her hand out to me, "What's troublin' ya, love?"

I stand and take her hand. I can touch it! Feel it. As real as my own hand.

"Will you be havin' a dance with me?" she asks.

"I'd love one," I say. I put my arm around her waist. I feel her move beneath her dress. She is so free. Nothing holds her in, back. She is a goddess, a queen. My love.

"Sweetheart," she says, as our dresses swish across the floor, "this is your last night. It is supposed to be a celebration."

"You know about me?"

She laughs. The world shifts as always when she laughs. I recognize her laugh.

"Of course I know about you," she says.

She laughs again. I *know* that laugh—I *remember* her laugh. It is my own. My laugh! She smiles as we dance. It is myself I see in her eyes: It is myself I have always seen in her eyes.

I step away from her and she smiles.

"That's it, sweetheart," she says. "You'd just forgotten who you were and who you are." She touches her lips gently to mine, and then she is gone and the house is quiet. I twirl around the empty room, smiling, laughing. I am in love with myself. Finally.

Nov 1, 1994

I cry and kiss the cat good-bye. Millie giggles as she hugs me, and I laugh. I wave good-bye to the house and all my ghosts. The cat watches me drive away. I am ready to go home: I am myself again.

A Christmas Caroler

"Nonsense, Benjamin," I said. "I do not believe in ghosts. I do not care how many ignorant people claim to have seen one."

"I would hardly call Adam Carroll ignorant, Charles," Benjamin said. He leaned against the mantel as he warmed a glass of brandy in his right hand. If I were a polite guest, I would have asked who Adam Carroll was. Instead, I stretched my legs until my feet nearly touched the fire.

Outside, another Pacific storm was beating against Seattle's shores. I could almost hear the ships moaning in Puget Sound as the wind lashed their sides and pulled at the moorings. As far as I was concerned, this was not a proper way for a civilized person to spend Christmas Eve. Although I had spent thirty Christmases on this earth in a variety of places, this particular place seemed the most loathsome. I had tolerated too much rain, too much greenery, and too much secret laughter between my sister and her childhood friend, Benjamin Jerome's wife. I longed for a true New England Christmas, away from this western wasteland. We had taken the buggy out the day before for a Christmas ride and had to turn back minutes later in order to keep from drowning in this foul weather.

"Carroll is an old and respected name in Seattle," Benjamin said. "I met him when I was quite young. By accident, really. I got caught out in another Christmas storm, similar to this one, actually."

I heard laughter coming from the drawing room. The door opened and my sister Gwendolyn leaned her head inside.

"Would you gentlemen like to play bridge?" she asked.

"No, darling, much as I enjoy the company of you two beautiful women, Benjamin is in the middle of a fascinating story," I said. "You two run along."

"As you wish," she said. "Good evening, Benjamin."

"Good evening, Gwendolyn," Benjamin said. He smiled when the door shut. "I thought you weren't interested in my tall tales."

"I am even less interested in bridge," I said. "Please continue."

"I had been on my way to a Christmas celebration and I got lost. Finally, I reached an old mansion sitting up on a hill in what seemed the middle of nowhere, though I was definitely in Seattle," he said. "I pounded on the huge wooden doors until an old servant opened them and beckoned me inside. I was concerned about my horse, but the man assured me someone would take care of it. He led me down a long dark hallway to a large room lit only by a roaring fire. The flames threw strange contorted shadows on the white sheeted furniture. Only the area near the fire appeared to be in use. Three chairs and a tea table ware arranged near the fire. I was shaking from the cold. I had been out in the storm for hours, after all, riding up and down long rutted drives and roads which led nowhere. The servant took me to a wing-backed chair closest to the fire. I sat down gratefully. I was so tired and cold and wet that I let the poor man pull off my boots.

"'I will get you something to eat,' the servant said. I didn't answer. I leaned back in the chair and closed my eyes. I was barely a man, you must understand, hardly versed in the ways and etiquette of the world, especially the ways of the Pacific Northwest. It seemed like such a different world from the one to which I was accustomed, after a child's lifetime in Boston. I was left alone in this huge room, not certain what to do. After a time I stopped shivering and began to notice my surroundings. My eyes had adjusted to the lighting, and I now saw that the walls were lined with books. I was in a library. I had never seen one quite so massive in anyone's home before. Outside, the storm was growing worse. Occasionally the wind reached such proportions that it shook the house. The windows rattled so violently that I was certain they would break. Yet, just as I thought the glass would burst, the wind lessened slightly and the windows remained secure.

"Finally, the old servant returned with a tray which he put on the tea cart near my chair. Steam rose from chowder, fresh bread, and a pot of tea.

"'You have been so kind,' I said. 'I would like to thank the master of the house as well.' I reached for the bread and dunked it into the chowder like a farmer because I was so famished after my ordeal.

"The servant laughed quietly. I looked over at him, truly seeing him for the first time. He was not as old as I had thought, merely somewhat frail and bent over. His hair was long and white. His skin was pale and smooth and appeared fairly untouched by the seasons. His blue eyes twinkled. Ah, you laugh now, Charles, yet I will say it again: His eyes did twinkle. Although his dress was sloppy, I could now see that he was no servant. I quickly rose to my feet and held out my hand.

"'I am sorry, sir,' I said. 'I am Benjamin Jerome at your service, sir.'

"He shook my hand and waved to me to be seated. 'I am Adam Carroll, sole owner of this old house. I am also sole resident of this house on this night. Even the servants are gone. Now you eat and rest. I will check on your mare again.'

"'Oh, please,' I said, starting to rise again. 'I cannot allow you to wait on me.'

"'Nonsense, son,' he said. 'My calling is to wait.'

"Then he was gone, swallowed by the shadows, or so it seemed at the time. I began eating. The chowder was the finest I had ever eaten, the bread the freshest. After I finished eating, I felt more like myself. I lounged in the chair and drank the tea. It was a very strong brew, the way only the English or the dead can drink it. Mr. Carroll was gone for a long while, and I was anxious for him to return. The winds had quieted. I put on my boots, now dry and almost brittle. I would need to oil them when I got home. I am revealing these minute details to you for a purpose. You must understand that I was fully conscious during the events which followed. As I was examining my boots, I slowly became aware that I was humming a Christmas carol, and I was not humming it alone. I straightened up.

"'Hello,' I called. The humming ceased. I shrugged away my discomfiture. I had heard the wind coming through a broken pane of glass, that was all. I sat down again to await my host. The sound began again, softly at first, and then louder: It was a little girl's voice. I sprang to my feet and looked behind me. There was a sudden flurry—how else can I explain it? As if snow had fallen in that spot for a moment and then disappeared. I was suddenly bitterly cold. I moved closer to the fire and wondered where Mr. Carroll was. Perhaps I had imagined him, also. Had I wandered into the house in a delirium?

"No, I shook my head decisively. It was all real. There was the teacart, the empty bowl, the tea cup with tea leaves stuck to the bottom, promoting some destiny I was unable to discern.

"Mr. Carroll returned suddenly. First I saw shadow, and then I saw Carroll. 'I apologize for being gone for such a long while,' he said. 'The horses were most upset by the wind. I cannot imagine why. They have lived with it all of their lives.' He warmed his hands in front of the fire. 'Are you comfortable and rested?'

"'Yes, certainly,' I said. 'But I have strained the bounds of neighborly hospitality long enough. Perhaps I should be on my way.'

"'I know spending Christmas Eve with an old man in an even older house is not very exciting for a young man such as yourself,' he said, 'but going abroad again tonight would be much too dangerous. Please, spend the night. You can join your friends in the morning.'

"'Thank you kindly, Mr. Carroll,' I told him.

"As we sat before the fire, we talked briefly about the weather. Then I became bold and said to him, 'I hope you won't think me rude, sir, but I cannot help wondering why a man as well-respected and well-known as yourself should be alone on Christmas.'

"He laughed. 'I am not alone. You are with me!' He pulled out his pipe, tapped it on the chair, and then began filling it from his pouch. 'This is the way I have spent each Christmas Eve for the past ten years.'

"'May I inquire why?'

"'I am waiting,' he said. He lit the pipe and drew on it several times before smoke rose from it. 'I have been waiting for my sister, Maureen.' He paused and looked at me. 'She has been dead these forty years.'

"Remember, Charles, I was aware of Adam Carroll's reputation; I was ready to listen objectively to whatever he had to say.

"'The last Christmas our entire family spent in this house was forty years ago,' he continued. 'My mother, father, Maureen, who was then ten years old; Daniel, my older brother; myself, I was twenty; and Patrick, who was only a few years younger than myself.

"'We were having a gay holiday. A great deal of eating and

singing and carrying on. I am afraid that Maureen was rather ignored in our family of males. She was young and somewhat frail. She wanted to tag along with her older brothers, but we were more interested in other things, much as you are at your young age. Quite a few young people from the area had gathered in this library to go caroling. Maureen was here, too. She kept singing this particular carol, trying to get the words right. I remember Patrick teasing her about it, saying she was a little idiot because she could not get the words right. Mother hushed him. We were stupid, loathsome boys. You just don't think when you are that age. I laughed at Maureen with the others. Finally, we were ready to leave. Maureen wanted to go with us. We said no and promised to listen to her carol later. She was deeply disappointed. We went out to the wagons. Just as we were about to leave, Maureen came running out of the house calling to us to wait. She startled the horses. Daniel could not get control of them. They reared and ran ahead, mad, the way horses sometimes get, and they ran her down. She died in my arms, on the muddy ground, whispering something I could not understand.'

"He was silent for a moment, gazing into the fire.

"'How awful,' I blurted.

"'Yes, Mother was grief-stricken. She died months later of some unknown ailment. My father hung on until the next Christmas, Then he died, but not before he gathered us all around his bedside and told us we were a cursed family. Maureen had visited him, he said, and death had changed her. She cursed the entire family. We were more devastated by this news, I believe, than we were by his death.

"'Daniel and Patrick were determined to forget everything my father had said. A relatively peaceful year passed. We had a party here on Christmas. In the middle of the night, I heard a scream. I ran out of my room to find several people gathered around the prone figure of a young woman at the bottom of the stairs. She said someone had pushed her, a young girl. There were no young girls at the party. My brothers were convinced now that my father was right: Maureen was haunting us.

"'Patrick went away to college, and I became involved with a woman I would someday marry, Jane Reilly. Daniel began drinking and gambling heavily. He stayed in this house alone the next Christmas Eve. I was at a party at Jane's, but I did try to get back here afterward. I had to turn back because of the weather. When I finally got home, I found Daniel, dead, stabbed through the heart in that very chair where you now sit. He left a note: She was here. There was an investigation and it was determined that Daniel had owed a great deal of money to some very shady characters. One of they had come to collect. They never arrested anyone.

"'I moved out and married Jane. We lived in a house her parents had built for us. Patrick returned from college and moved into this house. We invited him to live with us, but he wanted to stay here. Jane and I planned a lavish Christmas Eve party that year. We invited my brother, of course. He was the only family I had left! When he didn't show up, I rode over to the house. It was early morning by that time. He was in this room, my younger brother, his hair white, his cloudy blue eyes opened wide in terror. The doctor said he died of some kind of horrible fright. I buried him and closed up the house. For the next twenty years, I worked hard to forget about Maureen, to forget what had happened to my family.

"'Then, ten years ago, I decided I had been a coward long enough. If we had truly been responsible for little Maureen's death, then she had a right to exact vengeance. So every Christmas, I return to this place, alone, and I wait for Maureen. This is the tenth Christmas and she has not come yet.' He sighed deeply.

"I hesitated and then I said quietly, 'Sir, she was here.'

"'What?'

"'When you went out to take care of my horse, I heard someone singing, a young girl, I thought. Then I saw something, a kind of ghost of a shadow.' I laughed awkwardly. 'Sorry, sir, I don't mean to be flippant.'

"Carroll was silent. He looked stricken. The fire turned the tears in his eyes red. 'I have missed her once again,' he said mournfully.

"I was puzzled. I thought he would be relieved to have missed her. When his brothers had seen her, they had died. Carroll had been courting death for ten years. Now he was to survive one more year.

"'I want her to rest in peace,' he replied to my unasked question.

"The storm suddenly increased in intensity. We both looked toward the far window, which was rattling the most. When we turned back, the fire had almost died out. I sat up straight in my chair. I was cold; my bones ached. I was terrified! I did not want to meet this monstrous sister. I saw a flurry between our chairs, a whirlwind of snow, of particles trying to take shape, until they barely suggested the outline of a young girl. Carroll clutched his chest. 'Maureen,' he whispered.

"She began to sing. Her voice was lovely, high-pitched, slightly off-key, singing with all the enthusiasm of a ten year old girl. My fear evaporated as she sang the first verse and then the second. She sang each word and note carefully. Then she finished. She floated before us, silently, like a puff of smoke about to be blown away.

"'I remembered all the words,' she said. 'I knew I could do it.'

"Carroll reached out a hand to the girl.

"'I only wanted you to hear that I finally got all the words," she said. She seemed to smile. 'That was all, brother dearest. Live in peace."

"The wind shook the house. Maureen disappeared as the

flames in the fire leapt up the chimney. Adam Carroll wept silently. After a time, he came over to me and shook my hand.

"'Thank you, son,' he said. 'It has been a most enlightening evening. Now I think we should retire.' He took me upstairs to a bedroom, and I spent a peaceful night.

"We remained friends until he died a few years ago. On his death bed, he took my hand, squeezed it, and admonished me to always be kind to my sisters. By that time, I had fallen in love with and married his granddaughter, Merry. We moved into this house and have lived here happily for five years." Benjamin stretched out his arms, his tale completed.

"And Maureen? Does she finally rest in peace?" I asked.

"Benjamin." Merry came into the room. "Are you telling that ridiculous ghost story again? Charles, you mustn't pay any attention to him. He has made it all up. Every word. He and my grandfather loved to tell tall tales. Was it the brother haunting the sisters this year or little Maureen haunting her brothers? Ben, really!"

Benjamin smiled. Gwendolyn came in and bent over to kiss my cheek. "It's because my brother has been such a bore about the weather," Gwen said. "Christmas makes him tiresome."

I stood up. "Well, sir," I said, "it was indeed a fine story."

"It was a long story!" Merry said. "The children are going to be up very early, and we haven't even gone to sleep yet."

"All right, love," he said. "Let us retire."

"I think I shall stay up for a while," I said. "Good night all."

"In the morning then," Benjamin said.

"Good night, brother," Gwendolyn said.

They left me alone behind closed doors. I listened to their muffled voices as they climbed the stairs to bed. I sat in front of the fire and pulled out my pipe. I started to light it when suddenly the fire nearly died and the room became cold. Then I heard the sound of a young girl singing. I was paralyzed with fear. I dropped my pipe and gripped the armrests. I wanted to race out of the room or call for help, but I remembered the dead Carroll brothers, killed by their own guilt and fear. I remained motionless. I listened to the child's voice, high-pitched and off-key, sing an old Christmas song. Just as she finished the second verse and I was about to turn around, to face the child's ghost, the library doors flew open.

"Brother?" I started at the sound of my sister's voice. "What tune were you humming?" she asked.

"Oh, something I heard as a child," I said. I looked around the room. Little Maureen was nowhere in sight. The fire grew stronger and the room warmer.

"Would you like me to teach you the words?" I asked. I stood and put my arm around her waist.

"You? Charles, you are too impatient. You would have me in tears in minutes."

"I promise, sister," I said. "I will be patient and listen until you have every word memorized!"

We left the library together. Before I closed the doors, I leaned my head inside the now cozy room.

"Merry Christmas, Maureen," I whispered.

Hauntings

Kate awakened to the sound of her name being whispered in her ear, to the feel of warm breath on her cheek. She let the dream ebb away, taking with it the sound and warmth before she opened her eyes to darkness.

"Kate," the whisperer said again, sighing, settling and creaking as all houses do in the quiet of night.

Still not fully awake, Kate switched on the light over her bed. Eerie shadows gave way to reveal her ordinary bedroom: faded peach wallpaper, painted ceramic light fixtures, jeans and shirt strewn on a chair, a black and white television set. The sound was gone.

She took a drink of water from the glass that was always on the night stand. She drank a great deal of water now, as if it could wash her clean if she drank enough of it. She yawned and settled back against her pillow. The whispering didn't frighten her. She had grown accustomed to the occasional noises in the two weeks she had lived in the nineteenth century farmhouse. They were almost company to her.

Except now they were disturbing her sleep even more than usual. She liked her time in her dreams. In them, she was usually well, whole; no one had taken a knife to her, no one had injected poisons into her.

She turned the light off. In the morning, she supposed, she'd have to find out why the house talked to her.

"Can I help you find anything, Mrs. Hein?" the librarian asked. Kate looked up and smiled. Everyone in Canyons insisted on calling her Mrs. even though her last name was different from her husband's. All they knew was that she was married, so she was Mrs. Hein to them.

"Call me Kate, please," Kate said, closing the book in front of her. "Maybe you can help. Do you know anything about the Nelson farmhouse?"

"You mean the house you bought?" he asked, sitting down next to her. On this sunny Monday afternoon, the library was empty except for Kate and the librarian. "It's been researched extensively by our historical society—of which I am a member. It hasn't been declared a historical landmark or anything—not architecturally unique enough—but it is one of our older homes. The society has pictures of it and of the people who lived in it. Their office is just across the courtyard."

"Before I bought it had the Nelsons always owned it?"

He shook his head. "It was built by a family from back east in the 1890s. They had money and decided to come here and get back to nature."

"People were doing that back then, too, eh?" Kate said, laughing. One of the reasons she had moved to Canyons was because there was no industry, no waste dumps, and plenty of land to grow her own food.

"I can't remember their names, something simple though," he said. "They owned it for about fifty years. Then they sold it to a distant cousin and moved back to New York. This cousin married a Nelson and it stayed in their family after that. They over-farmed the land, though, and they couldn't make any money, so they finally left. It was up for sale two years before you bought it."

"Any rumors of unusual happenings?" Kate asked.

The librarian glanced at her books *Poltergeists* and *Hauntings*.

"Nary a word," he said, "and I would have heard. It seems it was quite a happy home."

"Any Indian burial grounds nearby?"

The librarian laughed and stood up. "Nope. We didn't have Indians in that area. You're going to have to settle with just your run-of-the-mill ordinary house."

"Thanks." She turned back to her stack of books and magazines, and he went back to the check-out counter. Leafing through one of the magazines, the headline "Laetrile: Hope of the Future" caught her attention. She quickly turned the page. She never wanted to see another cancer article. When she had first found out she had cancer, she had read them all—after the initial frightened vomiting ended and the terrified night sweats lessened in frequency. For a time, she had thought about going the "natural" route, healing with foods and state of mind. In the end, she decided she couldn't trust her mind not to make the disease worse, so she had allowed surgery and chemotherapy.

She pushed away from the table and quickly left the library. Anger whirled around her as she stepped into the sunshine; the anger swelled in her and turned into fear. They said she was free of cancer now. What did they know? In twenty years when she was just over fifty, she would probably get cancer from the chemo and have to go through it all over again. She shivered and pulled the sweater closer to her. The house. She had to concentrate on the house. She crossed the courtyard and went toward the historical society office.

"Can I come for a visit soon?" Jeff asked over the phone. "It's been two weeks, Katie. I miss you."

"I thought you had an assignment," Kate said. She pulled the long telephone cord around with her as she walked from one end of the huge farm kitchen to the other. It was an uneconomical space, but the painted blue walls and the Dutch ceramic tiles made her feel cozy. The white cupboards stretched to the ceiling and Kate envisioned shelf upon shelf of Kerr canning jars filled with peaches, apples, tomatoes.

"Winter has set in there early this year," Jeff said, "so they cancelled it until spring."

"Spring?" Kate said, taking the tea kettle off the burner. The piercing whistle slowly hiccoughed to a stop. "That's six months."

"Yeah," he said. "Maybe by then you'll want to come back to work. Hint, hint."

Kate stopped moving. "I'm through, Jeff. Period. I like it here." There was silence on the other end. "Whatsamatter, don't you like your new partner?" she joked.

"He's not fun to cuddle with and he's not my partner," he said. "You and I are still under contract."

That much was true; they owed their publisher three books. She had been writing the texts and Jeff had been taking the photographs for their travel books since before they left college. They had just started branching out into more naturalistic settings (versus tourist spots) when Kate had gotten sick.

"I love you," he said. He sighed. "If you still need time alone, I understand."

She bit the inside of her cheek so she wouldn't cry. They had never been apart for this long, and even though it was her choice and it was temporary, she missed him.

"Come this weekend," she said.

Kate liked the house. In some ways it reminded her of her childhood—though when she really thought about it, she knew it was her father's childhood it reminded her of. She didn't want to think about her own past. What she had believed had been an idyllic child's life now seemed tainted with all the things that should have been done: Her parents should have fed her better foods, they shouldn't have put her through the stress of a custody battle when she was a teenager, and they should have known they lived two miles from the most toxic waste dump in the state. She leaned back in the chair, stretching her legs across the table. It made her too angry, the past, because there was not a thing she could do about it. It was just a compilation of "ifs".

The house shifted, and Kate let all thoughts of her past slip away. It was the house's past she was interested in now. The library and the historical society had not given her any clues as to why the house made noises; perhaps the house itself could.

"The attic," she said, dropping her feet from the coffee table and standing up. She glanced out the window at the fading light, wondering if she wanted to go into the attic at night, especially the attic of a haunted house. Heroines of horror novels were often doing things just like this and she'd always thought they were a bit stupid. She laughed; the sound vibrated around her, as if the walls were enjoying the sound. Kate was not afraid of the house, and she was not a heroine.

The attic was brightly lit by a line of fluorescent lights a previous owner had installed. Except for a work table and several boxes strewn in different corners, the room was empty. What little there was of Kate's things was still downstairs. Between buying the house and maintaining an apartment in the city, they had had little money left over for her to buy furnishings.

Kate knelt on the floor and began examining the boxes. Two of them were filled with moth-eaten clothes. Another box contained homemade Christmas decorations.

"Bingo," Kate said as she opened the last box and began taking out papers. Twenty-year-old grocery and utility bills. She dug deeper and found several letters. All were newsy, chatty letters from relatives asking the Nelsons about their rural life. At the bottom of the box were three letters written by Agatha Nelson to Aunt Betty Carens which had never been mailed: "The new calf is doing better. . . . We need rain. . . . The cows got loose in the alfalfa patch and gorged themselves." Folded in with Agatha's third letter was a faded page written in someone else's hand: '. . . Look what I found in the attic," Agatha had written. "Nellie Smith was one of the original owners. Please return this to me . . ."

Smiths and Nelsons. The all-American farmhouse. Nellie Smith's letter was like a piece of a diary, addressed to no one in particular. She described the farm and then the house: "The house is completed now, and we are settled in. I love it here away from the city. It is still in this house as if there is no past or future, just now—or as if it were all one time and what happened or will does not matter . . ."

Kate smiled and tucked the letter into her pocket to show to Jeff later. Perhaps one day she would develop Nellie's philosophy and none of it would matter to her either. She switched off the lights and went down the stairs.

"You're too ordinary," Kate said. "Maybe that's why you're haunted."

She brought herbal tea and peanut butter cookies up to her bedroom and turned on a romantic comedy from the fifties. She skimmed through the book on hauntings. It told her nothing new. Dead people haunted houses. Period.

She snapped the book shut and opened the one on poltergeists. They were usually short-term phenomena revolving around one person, often a troubled adolescent. It had not occurred to her that she could be causing the sounds, that perhaps it was all in her head. She was not a troubled teenager, but she was not a particularly happy adult.

When Kate awakened that night, the only noise she heard was coming from the marsh pond over her back hill. She sat up and drank from her glass. The clock read 2:45.

Feeling irritable, Kate got out of bed and went downstairs. She had not slept through an entire night in nearly two years.

She took an orange from the refrigerator and went into the living room and sank into her chair. Through the open curtains, she could see the back yard, touched with a bit of fairyland by the moonlight. "Kate," the room whispered.

Kate sat up straight and looked around the room. It was bathed in a white glow—moonlight—and something else in the middle of the room. Shimmering half there and half not was a woman. Kate blinked. The woman appeared to be sitting, her arms outstretched, her hands flat against something. Her image wavered, and Kate thought she saw someone else sitting, next to her. The image faded and was gone.

Kate sat very still for a long while. When the clock chimed four, she went back upstairs.

The next morning, Kate was still not frightened, and it puzzled her. Normal everyday Janes did not see ghosts. Perhaps the chemo had fried her brain a bit, or it had opened it up for new experiences. She took a long walk on her property and then spent the rest of the day putting the house into order. She could hardly wait until it was dark.

After supper, she read a book to put her to sleep and was not surprised to come awake just before 3:00.

She hurried downstairs and sat in her chair, waiting for the woman in white, concentrating only on seeing her. Then, as if it were quite natural, the woman was there again. This time, as she came into view, Kate saw she really wasn't wearing white. There was just a glow around her body. The image wavered and solidified. Five people sat around a table, their hands joined. She didn't recognize any of them from the photos she'd seen of the Smiths and Nelsons.

"Kate? Are you there?" the whisperer said. The woman looked up, her head moving as if in slow motion, the white glow shaking and then becoming still when she stopped.

They looked as though they were having a seance. Kate remembered holding seances on overnight camping trips when she'd been a Girl Scout. It had been an excuse to giggle and scream. These people looked quite serious. And they were calling her? It couldn't be. They were the ghosts; she was alive. It had to be another Kate. Hesitating, Kate got up from her chair and moved closer. "I can feel something," one of them whispered, the words floating through the house like a breeze through autumn-dried leaves. "Kate, if you're there, give us a sign," the dark-haired woman said. Kate giggled, a Girl Scout again.

"I am here," she said.

The woman nodded, as if she'd expected it all along.

"How are you, Kate Hein?" the woman asked.

Startled, Kate stopped walking around the circle.

"What? How?"

"Don't be frightened," the woman said.

"Ask her about Jenny. Have you seen my daughter Jenny? She's been dead three weeks," said another woman.

"Let me—" the dark-haired woman tried to interrupt.

"Can you tell us what it's like? Being dead?" a man asked.

Kate backed up and crashed into a table. Five heads turned toward her. "Look, there she is."

Someone screamed. The clock began chiming. The image faded away.

Kate breathed deeply, listening to her heart. The house's silence pounded her ears. Her cotton night shirt felt soft against her skin. Her mouth was dry. And she felt the floor firmly beneath her. She saw the moon outside. She had to be alive. She pinched her arm; it hurt.

What was happening? Had she died on the operating table and this was hell? No, it was too pleasant. Maybe heaven. This was what it was like to die and you never found out unless someone summoned you via a seance.

She ran to the phone and dialed her apartment.

"Jeff? It's Kate. Jeff, you've got to tell me. Did I die when I was operated on?"

"What?" he asked sleepily. "What are you talking about? Are you all right? Of course you didn't die."

"How do you know?" she asked, and then realized he wouldn't know if he was part of it all. This was crazy. Impossible. There had to be another reason.

"I'll leave now, Kate, and be there tomorrow night," he said.

She didn't object. She told him to drive carefully and hung up the phone. Sitting in the kitchen, she listened to the birds come awake one by one.

She didn't want to work anymore. She had told Jeff that during the treatments.

"I want to live in the country and enjoy life," she said. "All I'll need is food, and I'll grow my own."

"Why can't we live in the country and work, too?" Jeff had asked.

"I didn't say we," she said. "I'm not going to make you live in the country. You'd hate it."

"How can you know that when I don't?"

One thing about her past she wouldn't change was Jeff. He had always been there when she needed him, always supportive. When she had gotten sick, she found herself moving away from him, half angry with him all the time.

Now she wished he would get there. She looked out the window again. It would be dark soon, and she didn't want to be alone, didn't want to think she was dead.

There had to be another explanation. She thought of the dark-haired ghost woman and her companions, trying to remember everything: Perhaps details would help her. The woman asking after Jennifer had worn a red smock that matched her bright red hair; the dark-haired woman had on jeans and a sweater; one man looked as if he had on a robe. She couldn't see their faces clearly enough to describe them. The table had a shiny surface, perhaps glass, reflecting the light of a single candle. Were they people from another part of the world, their thoughts linked with hers?

That did not explain why they thought she was dead.

Jeff's car rolled across the gravel driveway. Looking concerned, he got out of the car and ran toward the house. She opened the door, and they embraced. He smelled of Jeff, a warm musky smell that made her hold him tighter.

"I missed you," she said.

He pulled away and looked down at her.

"Are you all right?" he asked.

"Come on in. I'll tell you all about it."

She related her experiences while they sipped tea and ate brightly colored salad, losing some of her fear as she talked. Jeff took the story at face value, just as she knew he would.

"So you thought you were dead?"

She grimaced and then smiled. "I never overreact, do I?"

"Oh no," he said. "When you found out you were sick, you called to have your tombstone made the next day."

"Luckily I decided not to tempt fate," she said, laughing. "Let's come downstairs tonight and see if you can figure out what is going on. Are you up to it?"

"I'll go to sleep after I eat, and you can wake me when it's time."

Kate put Jeff to bed, tucking him in as if he were a child.

"I left some things in the car," he murmured before drifting off.

Kate put on the floodlight and went outside. Inside the car were all of their plants, three suitcases, and Lockheart, their cat, asleep on a pile of clothes. She opened her eyes, meowed and stretched. Kate shook her head and picked the cat up. She protested at first; she was fond of the car, but she soon realized Kate was warmer.

Kate had not wanted the cat or the plants, and she felt a twinge of anger as she unloaded the car. They all required responsibility. Plants needed water; cats had to be fed. And people got sick and died. Of course, Jeff could not have called neighbors up at 3:00 A.M. and asked them to cat and plant sit.

Once inside, Lockheart sniffed at her litter box and food and then padded upstairs to sleep with Jeff. Just like home, Kate thought.

When she grew tired, Kate went to bed, curling herself around Jeff and the cat. At 2:30, she shook Jeff awake. They shut the door behind them and went down to the living room where they sat in the dark until it was almost three. Kate began to wonder if it would happen at all; perhaps she had made it up. Then the woman shimmered into view.

"Kate Hein, come back to us. We didn't mean to frighten you," the woman said. The others joined her.

"Do you see them?" Kate whispered. She was relieved when Jeff nodded; she hadn't made it all up.

Kate stood and went to them. Tonight she could see more details: a counter behind the table, a beauty mark on the man's left cheek, a window—her window.

"Give us a sign," the woman said.

Reaching into the light, Kate picked up a cup from the counter.

She couldn't feel it, but it moved and crashed to the floor. They all jumped.

Kate pulled her hand back. The clock chimed. She looked at Jeff, and the picture faded.

Jeff fumbled with the light and then sat down.

"Let me sit for a minute," he said.

Kate heard the cat crying upstairs. She went up and let her out.

"They looked different," Jeff said as she came down. "Didn't they? Their clothes. That room. It was like this one only a bit different."

"I know. The clothes weren't old-fashioned," Kate said. She smiled. "Not like I would have expected from ghosts."

"They did call to you," he said. "Maybe there's another Kate Hein somewhere."

"They're calling to her in this house? Doubtful," she said. "Why would they be in this room, in this house, calling me? Why do they think I'm dead? I'm not!"

"You will be someday in the future," he said, "in the far, far future."

"I'll be dead in the future. Yes, that's right," she said, suddenly excited. "I'm not dead now but I will be in the future, Jeff, so *they* could be from the future. Instead of holding a seance and getting the dead me, they get the past, with me in it."

"A kind of time travel?"

"I suppose," she answered, pacing the room. "Maybe in the future this house is haunted—strange noises in the night, things like that. Maybe I grow old and die here. They think I'm the one who is haunting the house, so they call me. To me the house is haunted, too, but it's haunted by the future! A window which goes both ways."

She laughed. "Think of it! Maybe many of the so-called haunted houses are really time windows—pieces of the future or past flickering back and forth with no one ever suspecting because both ends believe it's the nether regions."

"That's a better explanation than your first one," Jeff said.

Lockheart jumped onto Jeff's lap and he stroked her. "I wish there was one of these windows in the house I grew up in," Kate said, stopping to gaze across the yard.

Jeff sighed. "Why? So you could tell little Katie to eat right and move away from the dump? What would that have accomplished? Your parents would have taken you to a shrink and you would have grown up terrified of this woman who told you you would get cancer," Jeff said. "You can't change the past."

She walked across the room and dropped down on her knees in front of his chair. "But maybe I can change the future. Those people know who I am, for some reason; and in their time I'm dead. They could tell me why and how. I would know." She grabbed his hands. "I could stop being afraid. No more ifs."

"Katie," he said, cupping her face in his hands. "What does it matter? You can't live the future or the past. What if you find out I die in two years or you die a pauper or you win the Pulitzer or you live to be a hundred? Would you want to know any of those things ahead of time, really?"

She moved away from him.

"How can you understand? How can you sit there and pretend you do? You don't have a time bomb inside of you!"

"Is that why you've been so angry with me?" he asked. "Because I didn't get sick? Well, how do you know I don't have a 'time bomb' inside of me?" He started to leave the room. She reached for his arm.

"Don't you see? That's what I'm afraid of."

The house seemed even more warm and alive the next morning. Lockheart climbed along the counters while Jeff fixed breakfast.

"I tried the tractor again the other day," Kate said as they ate. "It still works. I wish it were spring so I could plant. All organic. I'll have complete control."

"I? Aren't you going to let me help?"

"It's something I want to do by myself," she answered. "Besides, I doubt you'll be here much of the time, will you? What would you do out here?"

"Eat what you grow," he said. "This is an interesting part of the state. We could do a back-to-nature book. I married you for better or worse. Don't the vows hold for both of us?"

"That's not nice," Kate said.

"I don't feel nice, Katie," he said. "I want to be with you, but only in the here and now, not with you angry about the past and worrying about the future."

Kate looked at her food and wished the night would come.

She moved slowly out of bed, trying not to disturb the cat or Jeff.

"Don't tell me," Jeff whispered. "Whatever you learn, I don't want to know."

She started to answer him, but instead she tiptoed out of the room and went downstairs. She sat in the chair waiting for her future and thinking about her past.

What she didn't like about the past was that she had no control of it. She had trusted the world to let her grow up unharmed, and it had failed her. Her doctor had told her she shouldn't blame her illness on any one thing: It was a combination of factors, nothing she could do about it now. She felt the anger ball in her. Nothing she could do now, but soon she would know her future and she would be prepared.

But would that give her more choices? Or would she just feel as if she were a puppet or actor playing out a role?

Was Jeff a part of her future? Jeff, the cat, and the plants the cat was always eating? She smiled. She liked the house better with them all in it.

The woman came into being in a milky glow, followed by the others.

"Are you there, Kate Hein?" the woman whispered.

"I'm here," Kate answered.

The people looked at each other and then warily about the room.

"Ask her," the other woman said.

"Kate, Mrs. Packard wants to know if you've had contact with her daughter Jennifer. Jenny passed away a short time ago."

Kate looked around the room. The plants made pointed silhouettes in the dark. Upstairs she heard Lockheart scratching at the door. Kate rubbed her stomach where she was still warm from Jeff's body pressed against hers as they slept.

"Tell Mrs. Packard that Jennifer is here with us, and she sends her love."

The clock struck three, and the window closed.

About the Author

Kim Antieau lives and writes in the Pacific Northwest. Her novels include *The Jigsaw Woman, Butch, Queendom: Feast of the Saints, Maternal Instincts*, and many others. Kim's non-fiction includes *The Salmon Mysteries: A Guidebook to a Reimagining of the Eleusinian Mysteries, Under the Tucson Moon*, and *Answering the Creative Call*. Learn more at www.kimantieau.com. She's also a photographer. Her photos can be found here: kimantieau.smugmug.com.